Acknowledgments

A special thanks to my editor, **Oliver Carter**, for the countless hours of work put into transforming the story you are about to read. Your patience and dedication to these characters have lifted my ideas into something I am truly proud of. Your suggestions and insight are instrumental to the progression of these characters into their future adventures.

Eternal Driftwood

Printed in the United States of America

ISBN: 9798986035253
Library of Congress Registration Number
TXU 2-365-289

First Edition: March 2023

Compass Heart Press LLC
Sacramento, CA 958

To Samuel

Every turn of life comes with its struggles. You have been dealt more than any one person should have to bear, yet you continue to push on. You live life with a passion that is nothing short of inspiring to those around you. I am eternally grateful to be one of the many people whose lives you have touched. Your kindness, support, and dedication have been integral to the success of some of my most cherished accomplishments. Your capacity to forgive and love your family, even in the face of personal struggles, is a truly angelic feat. You have set an example that will continue to inspire me for the rest of my life.

ONE

eads of sweat glistened on Nickelias' face, illuminated by the swirling array of colorful lights that spun above him. Each salty droplet trickled down Nickelias' face, pulsing in perfect synchrony with the beat of the music, as if dancing in harmony with its host. Dancing.

A heavy baseline thumped in time with the swaying and thrusting of his trim, taut body. As he spun around, Lias, as he was known to his loved ones, watched twelve other versions of himself dancing in rhythm with him. The ceiling-to-floor mirrors made the dance floor look crowded, even if he was dancing alone. Like a smoky house of glass.

Though tonight, he did not dance alone. Jonah—his roommate, his best friend, and his boyfriend—enjoyed the reprieve from responsibility in the company of Lias. Classes were out for summer, and the club was abuzz with locals from the 404, all celebrating and laughing, whooping and rejoicing alongside the young couple.

Familiar, smiling, intoxicated faces from the University of Georgia's campus filled every corner of the dance floor, pushing the couple closer together. Glistening faces shone with the oils that had accumulated from a semester of unhealthy eating, and exhausted eyes with dark purple bags beneath them from too much caffeine swayed with the rhythm.

Jonah's sculpted chest felt charged with static as the crowd pressed him closer to Lias. He felt out of his depth here; he much preferred the tranquil, secure atmosphere of their apartment to a night out on the town. Nothing in this room, except for Lias, held any appeal for Jonah.

Tonight, however, was not about Jonah. After completing another semester of classes with perfect grades, Lias needed to celebrate in the way *he* enjoyed.

As always, Jonah was there by his side, supporting him even though the club atmosphere sent shivers of anxiety up his spine. The stench of spilled liquor, hastily mopped up with sodden rags, along with excessive cologne and body odor, sent a wave of revulsion through him.

They had been dancing for hours, and the overcrowded dance floor was pushing Jonah's introverted personality to its limits. Strangers were constantly brushing up against him, and the growing crowd was becoming too much for him to handle.

Jonah's wide, emerald eyes wordlessly begged his companion, "Let's get out of here." Jonah's built arms pulled Lias close and firmly gripped his toned butt as further evidence of his plea to leave.

Electric waves and familiar tightening at Jonah's waists let him know he had been heard. He let his right hand drop from Lias' buttock to his thigh, lacing their hands together as he turned and led them off the dance floor. Jonah had to restrain himself from breaking into a run the second they were free of the crowd.

* * *

Lias lay on his side, transfixed by the sight of his exhausted partner bathed in the late morning sun. Jonah's lustrous copper hair was perfectly sculpted, his cheeks and chin lightly graced with a hint of charcoal scruff that never seemed to change. Not one hair was out of place. Despite the night of drinking, dancing, playing, and sleeping, Jonah's beauty was eternal.

"Stop that," Jonah grumbled without opening his eyes. "I can feel you staring. It's creepy."

"I wasn't staring," Lias replied. "I was admiring, debating how much longer I should let you sleep. We're meeting my parents for lunch, remember?"

"As if I could forget," Jonah said mockingly, playfully jabbing Lias with his foot. "I haven't missed a single Saturday lunch with them since we started college, have I?"

"No," Lias admitted, "but we did have a lot to drink last night. This could have been the day."

"Go get in the shower. I can smell you from here," Jonah said with a mischievous smile, tossing a pillow at Lias.

"That smell is your filth all over my body, you jerk!" Lias replied, flinging the pillow back at Jonah as he rolled out of bed in the opposite direction.

"That it is," Jonah agreed, his satisfied smirk lingering as he rolled over to sleep for a little longer.

Typical top, Lias thought, rolling his eyes as he walked into the bathroom to get ready for the day ahead. As he closed the door, his bare feet stepped onto the cold tile, and he flipped his hand around the wall to turn on the light. The blue swirls in the white, frozen tiles at his feet were a favorite part of this apartment, one of the only selling points that mattered to him.

Finding the perfect wall border print to complement the tiles was Lias' top priority when they moved in, even before unpacking. The bathroom took up most of his time, between handling the calls of nature and making sure he was groomed to perfection for his extraverted endeavors.

As the light came to life, Lias buried his eyes into the mirror, waiting for them to adjust to the brightness. There, scrawled on the bathroom mirror in dry-erase markers, was a shopping list in Jonah's messy handwriting. He read it over, taking in each item, as he prepared to start his daily routine.

Thanks to Jonah's strategic placement of the list in the one spot Lias was sure to look, he was able to avoid shopping like the plague. This passive-aggressive reminder was his way of saying, *I love you, but I can't possibly do this myself.* Lias brushed his teeth as he read through the list, preparing for the errands he would have to run later.

Soap, toilet paper, floss, mouthwash, condoms...

"Condoms," Lias read aloud, recalling the satisfied smirk on Jonah's face when he'd jotted down the item on the shopping list that morning. He shook his head, a faint smile playing on his lips as he mused, *Well, he'd better not get too used to not having them.*

The couple had been together since middle school, and Lias had no fear of catching anything—Jonah was faithful through and through. Growing up in the era of COVID, though, and with his father's questionable past, Lias appreciated the added protection that condoms provided, even if they weren't necessary. But last night had been a celebration, and Lias wasn't going to let practicalities get in the way of that.

After showering away the smells of booze and sin, Lias stood before the mirror with a damp towel wrapped around his waist. His honey-colored curls, usually so obedient, were a tangled mess from the night before. He ran his fingers through the knotted strands, trying to get them back into place, but the more he tugged, the more frustrated he got. He cursed his unruly mane and, as he did so often, threatened to shave it all off.

The scene made Jonah chuckle as he flung open the bathroom door, having come to investigate what was taking so long. This was far from the first time he'd witnessed this argument.

"Leave them be," Jonah commanded with a smile as he walked up to stand behind Lias, gazing into the mirror.

Jonah embraced Lias, clasping his hands together to form a heart on his partner's belly. As always, the corny gesture produced a peaceful smile on Lias' face. Jonah pressed his hands together against

Lias' velvety stomach and planted a kiss on his neck. The tender kiss was followed by a sultry lick, making Lias' skin tingle, and Jonah's palms began to drift further down.

Lias swatted Jonah's hands away, turning to face him. "No, we don't have time for another shower," he said, though his expression spoke of longing and desire.

"Are you sure?" Jonah asked, spinning Lias back to him and pressing forward with a passionate kiss on the lips, not giving him a chance to respond.

"I'm sure," Lias mumbled between Jonah's lips. "Get yourself in the shower, you smell like day-old party garbage."

Jonah broke off the kiss and stepped back, admiring the man he loved. "Let me help first," he said, reaching past Lias to pump conditioner into his palm. Pulling his hands back to his face, Jonah lightly rubbed them together for a second. He then cupped them together upright and blew his warm breath into his conditioner-filled palms before rubbing them together one last time.

Jonah slowly massaged the warm product into Lias' hair, probing at his scalp and bringing life back to each curl as his fingers touched them.

"Thank you," Lias said, followed by a kiss. Jonah always seemed to know exactly how to calm Lias when he got worked up over life.

"Now get in the shower," Lias commanded, "before we're late."

"Get in with me," Jonah smiled, dropping his underwear and stepping into the shower.

Lias thought for a moment, considering the invitation. However, the thought of messing up his freshly styled hair again made him hesitate.

"Not a chance," Lias chuckled, shaking his head. "Don't use up all the hot water."

TWO

Saturdays **were** a long-standing ritual for the two boys; a way of staying connected to their families ever since they moved in together. They cherished their families and, unlike many college students who relished newfound independence from parental control, their weekly routine remained the same. Every Saturday, they would have brunch with Lias' fathers, Matthew, and Samuel, and then visit Jonah's mother, Vivian, in the afternoon.

Today, their double date was at Maw Maw's country café; a favorite spot of theirs that was always bustling. The waiters were dressed in flannel long-sleeved shirts tucked into tight-fitting wranglers, and they were always ready with heaping helpings of biscuits, fried potatoes, and oatmeal. The air was permeated with the aroma of freshly churned butter, honey, and baked bread. Anyone leaving Maw Maw's not feeling completely stuffed had only themselves to blame!

Once they were seated, Lias excused himself; an occurrence that was not unfamiliar to the others at the table. Everyone knew that Lias had a small bladder. As soon as he was out of earshot, Jonah turned to Lias' parents.

"How were your finals?" Matthew asked.

"They were great, sir," Jonah replied. "It's very exciting to finish another year."

"Have you boys made any final plans for work after graduation next year?" Samuel queried.

"No, sir, not for work," Jonah answered. "But I do have some personal plans." His voice tightened as he spoke, and he quickly surveyed the room before continuing.

"Personally, you both know I love your son with all my heart. I always have, and I always will. Before he gets back, I wanted to ask for your blessing in asking Lias to marry me after graduation next year."

Matthew and Samuel exchanged a silent look that Jonah couldn't decipher. It wasn't anger, frustration, or joy, but rather a look of two people who had just observed something they had expected to happen but still had some reservations about.

"I promise I will take good care of him," Jonah pleaded, telepathically begging them for their blessing.

"Of course, you will," Samuel finally spoke up. "We have long since considered you as part of the family. And of course, you have our blessing."

"Please don't take our awkward exchange as anything less than pride," Matthew said, reaching out to shake Jonah's hand. "We've always known that you'd be joining our family. Even before you ask Lias, we know you'll be one of us. We just thought the conversation would take place further down the line, and we'd have more time to prepare for it."

Though the sentiment was sweet, and claimed a blessing, the inflection in Matthew's voice, and the way his gaze shifted around the room—as if he were waiting for an attack—did nothing to soothe Jonah's nerves. Taking a deep breath, Jonah continued.

"I love him, and I already know that I want to spend the rest of my life with your son," he said, with conviction.

"We know that," the dads replied in unison. Exchanging smiles, Samuel nodded for Matthew to carry on.

"We understand how it feels at a young age to see your future with someone so clearly," Matthew affirmed. "We have no doubt that the two of you are meant to be together, and we won't be making you wait until you're older."

Jonah returned the smile, quickly looking around the room to check that Lias hadn't returned yet.

"Thanks for understanding," he beamed. "My dad passed away when I was young, so I've always considered the two of you as my surrogate fathers."

"We feel the same way," Samuel added.

"Feel the same way about what?" Lias asked, suddenly appearing.

"We feel like the day's too beautiful to not go for a walk in the park after brunch," Matthew answered without missing a beat.

"I could really use some Vitamin C after last night," Jonah added, giving Matthew a secret wink of gratitude.

Okay," Lias declared, sitting down. "But if we're walking after this, I guess no carbs for me."

* * *

The fresh air and warm Georgia sun felt glorious on Jonah's skin. He was thankful that this meeting with his soon-to-be in-laws had taken place today. The conversation and connection he found with them was unlike any other. Yes, they were Lias' parents, but their weekly brunch was a source of rejuvenation for both Jonah and his partner. Their presence was natural, warm, and inviting—something Jonah always needed to recharge.

The remaining part of their day, however, always drained Jonah. He was unable to have a similar conversation with his mother, whose dementia made it difficult to understand him. He could say the same words to her but would never know if she comprehended.

It all had begun almost overnight during Jonah's freshman year of college. Being the last of his family, he had to make the difficult decision of placing his mother in a home that could provide her with full-time care. Fortunately, the money from the sale of his childhood home, his father's company, and his father's pension was enough to ensure that his mother would be taken care of for the rest of her life.

"What is the summer plan?" Matthew asked, bringing Jonah back to the present.

"Well," Lias began, "we both have some local commitments, but at the end of summer we thought it would be nice to visit Mama Jene down in the Florida Keys for a couple of weeks before school starts up again. We can take in the sun and enjoy the beach."

"Very nice," Samuel said. "Be prepared for the crowds though—everyone wants to hit those beaches, especially in the summer months."

"The crowds are half the fun," Lias declared.

Jonah smiled and nodded, though he wasn't exactly looking forward to the crowded beach, which was the first thing Lias mentioned. Jonah was always ready to support his partner and jumped on the bandwagon to make sure Lias was happy. Jonah wanted a private beach getaway with his boyfriend.

* * *

Vivian was sitting in her usual, squeaky rocking chair, facing out the window. The sun's diminishing rays danced across her still-youthful skin.

"Hi, Mom," Jonah said, crossing the room and kissing her on the cheek.

"Is that you, Tommy?" she asked.

Jonah let out a familiar, defeated breath. His heart sank, as it did every time his mother failed to recognize him—the only blood relative he had left in the world. Even though his soon-to-be fiancé stood nearby, whenever his mother didn't know him, Jonah felt utterly alone. "No, Mom, it's me—Jonah," he answered.

"Hello, Vivian," Lias said softly, joining Jonah at her side.

Vivian adjusted her gaze from her son to the new man, and a warm smile spread across her aged face. "Lias, my dear," she said. "How are you? How are the kids?"

Lias, who visited weekly with Jonah, was used to Vivian not knowing them, confusing them with other people, and asking unusual questions. He had developed the habit of engaging her in conversation, as if he understood her, which always seemed to make the interaction easier.

"They're still kicking," Lias said, with a boastful chuckle. Their voices echoed down the hallway, no doubt annoying some of the overworked orderlies.

"Well, when you see them," Vivian said, "tell them I was asking after them. You will do that, won't you, honey?"

"Of course, I will," Lias promised.

Jonah admired how natural Lias was at pretending that everything was all right and normal. Every week was different. Last week, she remembered him as the lion tamer from a zoo she'd visited as a child. Lias had sat with her for half an hour, describing his time living in a den with lion cubs in Africa, and how he'd gained their trust so they would behave for him during the show, which she'd loved to watch.

Another time, Vivian had mistaken Lias for one of her favorite actors on TV. He'd spent the afternoon telling her all about his move to Hollywood from

Atlanta and how no one had thought he'd make it out there. Lias shared how his biggest supporter had been his mother, and how Vivian reminded him so much of her. She'd been so enthralled with the story that she'd begged Lias to autograph some of her belongings, which he'd gladly done in his perfect penmanship.

She often called Jonah by a different name, but she never remembered him from another role in her life. Perhaps some part of her sensed that he was not capable of having the same type of conversation with her as Lias did. Jonah was thankful that Lias was always there with him. He often spent the whole afternoon just listening to their conversation without him, taking pleasure in the moments he shared with the two people he cherished the most, always getting along regardless of whom Lias pretended to be that day for her.

In the beginning, when she was first brought there, Jonah would try to visit her alone out of loyalty. But the interactions were too painful for him to endure alone. He spent countless hours on the front steps, pouring out his soul to the world, when she didn't even know who he was.

He always saw that she was as miserable as he was, even though she was unaware of her identity for the majority of the time. When he started allowing Lias to accompany him, moments of joy returned to her face.

"Tommy," she said, turning her attention to where Jonah sat on the bed. "Would you get the tea?"

Jonah stiffened, his heart aching as it always did when she addressed him this way. Every time she uttered something other than his name, the dread that she would never remember him again intensified.

"Don't worry about Tommy," Lias said, watching Jonah's body tense in response to the name. "It's been a tough week for him. He got into trouble at work for not paying attention. He was supposed to fill a customer's car with gasoline, but he mixed up the buckets and ended up filling it with suds. As the car drove away, bubbles went everywhere, and Tommy had to chase it down and mop up the mess."

Vivian let out a hearty chuckle. "That sounds like my Tommy," she said. "Always up to some kind of mischief."

"Tommy, would you like to go down to the kitchen and get our tea?" Lias asked, giving Jonah a hint that he should accept the earlier request from Vivian's imaginary character.

"Apologies, ma'am," Jonah said in his best mechanic's accent as he rose from the bed. "I'll head down there right away." As he passed the two, he leaned down and kissed Lias on the cheek.

Jonah let out a yelp as his mother's hand smacked against his cheek with a force that stunned him. His gaze, wide and brimming with tears, shifted to his mother as he brought his hand up to his stinging face.

"Tommy," Vivian cautioned, her voice stern. "You leave him be. He belongs to my boy Jonah."

"Yeah, Tommy," Lias snickered in agreement. "Don't you know I'm married?"

Fresh tears welled up in Jonah's eyes, not from the pain of the slap, but from the reminder that, even in her confusion, his mother still recognized that Lias belonged to him. It was enough to bring sunshine to what had otherwise been a dreadful day.

"My apologies, ma'am," Jonah finally said, dipping in a mock bow. "I didn't realize he was spoken for. Now that I've put my foot in my mouth, I'mma do my best to see to it you two are taken care of—tea and all."

Vivian nodded her approval and Jonah made his way to the kitchen and back with tea in hand. The short excursion gave him a chance to compose himself, something that always seemed to be a difficult job these days.

One of the downsides of watching his mom slowly lose her faculties was the fact that, come such time, he would be alone in the world, biologically, at least. In the meantime, however, he was blessed to have Lias and his family to turn to. The thought of being able to call his new family his own was enough to get him through the day.

When he returned, he was greeted by the familiar sight of his mother's gorgeous eyes.

"Jonah," Vivian started. "Thank God you're here. That Tommy was makin' a move on Lias here."

"What?!" Jonah cried, pleased to once again note that his mother still recognized him. Turning to face Lias, he said, "I've told that idiot before to stay away from what's mine."

"Better head over and speak with his folks," Vivian suggested, and Jonah agreed. He leaned in and planted a kiss on Lias, thankful that they could be together without fear of interruption.

"Yes, Momma," Jonah nodded. "I'll let them know their boy's been making moves where he shouldn't."

He then stepped back and asked, "Do you mind if I have a moment alone with her? I'll meet you out front."

"Of course," Lias replied, giving Vivian a peck on the cheek before leaving the room. Once they were alone, Jonah gave his mother's tea a stir before passing it to her. He then cleared his throat and began.

"Momma, I've gotta tell you something," he began, his heart thumping in his chest. "I want to talk to you without interference this time."

"What is it, baby?" she asked, her voice trembling as she watched her cup shake in his hand.

"No, nothing's wrong," he smiled, reassuring her. "Actually, it's something that's right but still terribly scary." Taking a deep breath, he finally said what he had been longing to say all day.

"Again?" Vivian gasped in gentle surprise.

Jonah shook his head in confusion as the sunlight streaming through the window shifted to oranges and reds, signaling the end of the day. Sadly, it was no surprise that her mind was also beginning to set like the sun.

"No, Momma," he admitted. "I haven't asked him. Why do you say again?"

"I remember," she stared, a faraway look in her eyes. "You two were walking hand in hand down the sidewalk under the shade of giant trees. The leaves danced around you like a song, and then you got down on one knee and proposed. It was so romantic—much better than any scene in a movie."

"Oh, right," Jonah realized, understanding now. No use arguing while she was still lucid. He was grateful that his mother had witnessed the idyllic proposal he wanted her to remember—one much better than the awkward one he was likely to give someday.

"My dear, you shouldn't forget something so important," she said with a smirk.

Jonah smiled, though his heart was heavy. He could only hope that this beautiful moment she had captured in her mind would last until the true one materialized.

THREE

Sliding against the cool wall, Jonah stepped out of his mother's room and was relieved to find the hallway empty. The visit had been an emotional roller coaster and he needed a moment alone before facing more prying eyes. He allowed his body to slide until he was sitting on the floor, savoring the silence while reflecting on the conversation they'd had.

So much in such a short time, Jonah thought. *She hadn't known me, then suddenly she did. She recognized*

Lias and even thought we were already married. Jonah smiled and wondered if, on the next visit, his mother could tell him more about the proposal she'd described. It was as if she had conjured up the perfect place for such a moment: a setting so beautiful and familiar it was almost palpable.

Firmly determined to get up, he stood and headed out, remembering his task: to find Lias before Tommy. Jonah chuckled, recalling the slap that his mother had given him before his departure. Despite being disconnected from the world, some part of her had been aware enough to look out for him and save Lias' honor.

* * *

Magnolia trees in full bloom lined the concrete walkway that led to the weathered sidewalk. Mottled shadows from the mighty trees stretched out along the path like leafy fingers as the boys walked away from Vivian's care center.

The ambrosial aroma of ripe honeysuckles hung heavily in the air. With every breath, Jonah's lungs filled with the honey-tinted air that exuded sweetness. Taking Lias' hand in his, Jonah led the way. Nothing more could have made the day any better.

A gentle breeze brought life to the hidden windchimes tucked beneath the grand trees, adding another layer of sound to the already enchanting scene. Overlapping harmonic melodies from the wood and metal chimes filled the air.

Goosebumps rose on Jonah's skin as all his senses were triggered by the grandeur of the moment. Something deep inside of him stirred as an invisible finger pointed out an odd connection—the perfect moment his mother had described earlier in the day.

Coming to a stop, Jonah turned to Lias and took a deep breath. He was equal parts prepared and petrified by the thought of what was on his mind. Still holding Lias' hand in his, Jonah sunk down to one knee.

"Lias," he said in a voice trembling with emotion, "today has been the most beautiful day I can remember in a long time. There's only one thing I can think of that would make it even more perfect. I wasn't expecting to do this today and I don't have a ring, but I do have a heart full of love to offer you. Will you marry me?"

Lias, taken aback and confused as to why Jonah seemed scared to ask the question, first took a moment to observe their surroundings. The walkway was now painted in warm oranges, while the sweet smell of candy perfumed the very air they were breathing. His gaze eventually returned to his boyfriend, whose eyes glistened with tears.

Jonah mustered all the courage he had, then continued. "I wanted to wait until next summer to ask you this, but this moment felt so right."

Lias took in the awe-inspiring scene before him and, as soon as Jonah had finished his sentence, recognized the sheer perfection of the moment and all the memories that it would contain.

The growing silence from Lias' lips sent trepidation of fear down Jonah's spine. *Does he need some time to think about this? Is this not as cut and dry as it appears in the movies? How long should I stay on my bent knee in silence? Don't break down, Jonah. Don't break down. Keep it together.*

Lias' eyes glimmered while the deep thoughts in his head whirled around.

"Yes, I'll marry you!" Lias suddenly screamed with a beaming smile stretching across his face. "Now get up and kiss me!"

"Yes?" Jonah asked disbelievingly as he stood to his feet.

"Yes, you idiot!" Lias joyously echoed with a giggle, grabbing each of Jonah's hands and leapt up and down in celebration. As their energy faded, they swayed in perfect harmony, dancing to the melody of the captivating soundtrack that filled their air, lips locked together until all the air had been taken from them, as if to prove that the feeling of this moment would never, ever dissipate.

"If you need more time I can wait a few weeks," Jonah finally said, reflecting on the initial moment of extended silence. "I can wait the rest of my life for you."

"No," Lias spoke fervently, "I don't need another second to know what I've been imagining for quite some time now."

"You've been imagining this for a while?" he inquired, his doubts still conquerable.

"But…" Lias breathed, leaning in close and right into Jonah's ear, "ring or not, I don't want to wait until next summer. If you know, if you are certain, you want me, then let's get married while everything is so perfect. Let's not wait another day."

This response was typical Lias—take a plunge, feel the sensation of having your feet wet, and then figure out if the waters are deep or if there's a current. Quite the opposite of Jonah, who preferred to check the weather and the conditions, investigating a bit before embarking on any kind of adventure.

"You really want to get married now?" he asked, returning to his original position yet keeping his arms securely locked around Lias' shoulders. "You're ready for that?"

"Yes. I've been ready to marry you since high school. We've spoken about this before. Why are you so surprised?"

"Well, I had no idea I'd be asking you tonight," Jonah confessed. "Today I went from being in a relationship to having a fiancé and soon, a husband. It's a lot to process, even though it's exactly what I've always wanted. What exactly do you mean by 'ready' now?"

Lias took Jonah by the hand and started pulling him along as they continued walking.

"Well," he said, "by now I mean let's go tell my parents they have to put together a wedding before we head off to Florida."

* * *

Electricity filled the Anderson household with excitement as the boys shared their news with Matthew and Samuel, as well as Lias' sisters, Eternity and Octavia, or Tavia as she was known to their closest friends and family. Glowing faces revealed the pleasant surprise that their family would soon grow.

"When you asked for our blessing," Matthew began with a mischievous twinkle in his eye, "we didn't expect it to be today."

"Sir," Jonah replied, "at the time, I didn't know when the right moment would present itself. But when I asked today, I knew the universe was speaking and I had to listen."

Matthew nodded in agreement, knowing full well the truth in Jonah's words.

"No more 'sir' nonsense," Matthew instructed. "When you're ready, you can call me Papa. Until then, Matthew will do just fine."

"Thanks, Papa," Jonah said quickly, savoring the sweetness of words he'd kept tucked away like a secret since his father's passing. Papa. Dad. Daddy. Words that had been forbidden fruit for so long. Yet at this moment, it was time for them to come out of their dusty retirement.

At the prospect of putting together a wedding reception in a few short weeks, Lias' rambunctious laughter filled the parlor. Suddenly, Matthew cleared his throat and the room fell silent.

"Lias," Matthew said firmly. "I believe you have a phone call to make."

"Me?" Lias questioned, puzzling over what phone call his father wanted him to make.

"Yes, son," Matthew replied. "Your brother will need all the notice he can get if you hope for him to make it."

Matswell was often off in some far-flung corner of the world searching for answers to questions that most people hadn't yet thought to ask. He lived the life of a starving artist—sometimes lucrative and sometimes not—but he rarely kept a home of his own. When in town he'd stay with their fathers or one of his siblings.

"I almost..." Lias began. His father subtly waved his hand in a shooing manner and Lias realized he needed to get moving.

"Samuel," Matthew continued, "why don't you and the girls go with him and put together a list of what needs to be done? Jonah, I'd appreciate it if you and I could chat for a bit. Before you become a part of this family, there are a few things we need to discuss."

Every shocked stare met Matthew with a silent but resounding question.

"Are you sure now is the time for that?" Lias asked, at a loss for what other option they had.

Matthew nodded with a reassuring smile. "Yes, now is the time."

FOUR

Jonah followed** Matthew up the winding staircase to the room at the summit. He knew its purpose well, but he rarely set foot inside. This was Matthew's study, and it was more like a miniature library than a study space. Floor-to-ceiling bookshelves encased the walls from left to right, and every inch was filled to the brim with texts. The smell of aged pages wafted through the room as Matthew closed the door behind them.

Ahead, an intimidating desk was covered in a perfectly chaotic mess of books, notes, and pads. Although Matthew's intelligence was never boasted, Jonah was aware of his capability, and it made him uneasy.

He quickly glanced away from the desk and to the window that spanned the wall, which overlooked the backyard he spent most of his childhood in. Matthew led them to the corner of the room, where a small table was almost magically hidden.

"Please come and sit with me, Jonah," Matthew spoke kindly, beckoning Jonah towards the two-person seating area. *Had that always been there?* Jonah wondered.

"I cannot thank you enough for allowing me to be a part of this family," Jonah stammered, filled with honor from the recent acceptance.

"We are just as ecstatic to have you," Matthew replied, handing him a bottle of chilled water. "Samuel and I have always thought of you as family, and it's plainly evident how much Lias loves you."

Though the conversation was civil, Jonah could not help but thump his eyes nervously, pleading with his mind to keep them afloat. *What could Matthew want to speak with me about so privately? Was this the part where he would warn me not to hurt his son, or else I'd 'face the consequences?'* Jonah immediately shook the thought away. He knew Matthew to be a person who valued logic and strategy over violence. This desk was not that of a wicked man.

"With all big decisions in life, it is important to research as thoroughly as possible," Matthew began as he noticed Jonah's anxiety. "Fill yourself in on the details, as they say. Learn everything you can."

"Yes, Papa sir," Jonah nodded.

"There's no cause to be scared," Matthew assured him with a smile. "This isn't a scene out of some dreadful movie you've seen on television. I simply wish to give you information that you would have no way of knowing about our family and its origins."

Jonah released a breath of relief when he heard Matthew's words and observed his relaxed body language. He thought to himself, *He isn't some crazy Godfather. He just wants to tell me the family history.* However, something in Matthew's mention of the "origins" of their family made Jonah pause, as if they were from some otherworldly source.

Matthew spoke softly, in an effort to keep Jonah at ease. "As you may or may not know, I met Samuel in high school in a small country town. Things were quite different back then, especially in the Midwest. People's mindsets were quite closed off, and there wasn't much interest in expanding them. Much like you, I knew from a very young age who I wanted to spend my life with."

Jonah smiled at the comparison, feeling proud to be compared to the man he looked up to. "Samuel, on the other hand, was a bit of a mess during those days. And, just between us, at times he still is." Matthew grinned. "Even though he knew he liked me, he didn't know how to make sense of it with his religious background."

"We kept our relationship a secret," Matthew continued. "Society had taught him what he was expected to want out of life: a home, stability, children with their father's eyes and their mother's smile." At the mention of sweet children, Jonah couldn't help but smile.

"Unfortunately, the pressure of the world's expectations became too much for him, and he eventually broke up with me in an attempt to be 'normal,'" Matthew revealed.

"That's awful, Papa," Jonah murmured, still surprised by the thought of his fathers-to-be breaking up.

"It's all in the past now, son," Matthew replied. "I wasn't about to give up so easily. Unlike Samuel, I was completely sure of what I wanted, and I wasn't ready to be pushed away that easily. Would you allow Lias to push you away so easily?"

"No, sir!" Jonah answered confidently, with more conviction than he had spoken with all night.

"Of course not," Matthew agreed. "When you know who you want, you don't let anyone stop you from having them, not even their own irrational thoughts.

Before that conversation with him, my life was all about music. All I wanted to do was play music. But, at that moment, I knew that if I wanted to be with him, I had to be able to provide a more stable life. So, I changed all of my classes to more advanced biology-related courses, which the small school was able to provide via ITV."

Jonah was captivated by Matthew's story. He had changed his entire life in an instant, in order to become what Samuel wanted and needed. Jonah perfectly understood this, as he often did the same for Lias, though usually not to such an extreme. He found himself leaning forward, wanting to ensure he didn't miss a single detail his Papa was now sharing with him.

"It took some time," Matthew continued, "but eventually, after some time apart, I was able to show Samuel that I could give him everything he told me he wanted in life. It was junior year of high school when I proposed to him. We remained engaged in secret for years."

Wow, Jonah thought. *Here I thought we were young.*

"As I said, I understand," Matthew said, noting the surprise on Jonah's face. "Biology came naturally to me, and it carried me all the way through Harvard. After college, we moved back to our hometown and into our first home together. I spent years there in private, doing some biological research of my own. I still had something left to give that I had promised Samuel."

Question marks hung in the irises of Jonah's eyes.

"Before I say anything further," Matthew began, "I want to make it clear that what I am about to tell you is my secret, not Lias'. While, after hearing it, you may feel like this is something he should have shared with you, it's just him holding onto his father's confidence. You can understand that, right?"

"Yes, sir, I can," Jonah answered. He loved and missed his father dearly, and he knew that if there was any secret between them, not even the NSA would be able to get it out of his lips. Whatever Matthew was about to tell him, Jonah knew that Lias' silence was a sign of devotion to his father; something he could understand fully.

"I thought you might," Matthew whispered. "I was researching experimental reproduction techniques in animals: all off the books, no company backing, no FDA approval."

Oh, Jonah thought, *Unapproved research. It's no wonder the family wouldn't want it made public.*

"After years of researching through multiple generations," Matthew declared, "I felt pretty confident. But I wouldn't recommend anyone else do this kind of private research without approval—the consequences for me and my family could be massive if anyone ever found out what I discovered."

Jonah nodded solemnly. "I would never—"

But Matthew cut him off. "Across multiple species of mammals and generations, I was able to produce offspring using genetic material from two male parents. The world—especially back then—wasn't prepared for that kind of breakthrough." As he finished speaking, Matthew fell silent, and a heavy tension filled the room.

"Wow," Jonah breathed, his eyes wide in awe. "That's incredible. Do you think the same process could work for humans one day?" The idea captivated him; he had always wanted to have biological kids of his own, but being gay, he never thought it was possible.

"I know it will," Matthew replied quietly. "I have four children who are living proof of it."
Jonah sat in stunned silence, replaying the words in his mind. *I know it will. I know it will.* He was struggling to process what Matthew had just told him. The other man waited patiently for Jonah to take it all in.

Eventually, coherent words began to form at Jonah's lips. "Are you saying all your kids are biologically yours and Samuel's?" he asked.

"That's right," Matthew confirmed. "It was the last thing I promised him when we were teenagers. I wanted to make sure he didn't have to miss out on any of the experiences in life he wanted, just because he chose to be with me."

He paused and looked Jonah in the eye. "You can see why this has to stay in the family, can't you? If it got out, all my kids would become guinea pigs for the government, or some mad scientist, or some religious nut."

"Yeah," Jonah whispered, his gaze dropping to the floor. His mind was swarming with questions, and his heart raced with fear of the unknown.

Matthew sighed softly. "Lias is no different from anyone else, aside from his genetic origin," he said. "There's nothing to fear. But it's important that you know all the facts before deciding you want to spend the rest of your life with him." Jonah stared out the window into the inviting backyard, and they sat in silence for a few minutes.

"Are you okay?" Matthew asked eventually.

"Is this the look you and Samuel—Dad—were sharing when I asked to marry Lias today?" Jonah asked, recalling the moment.

"Yes," Matthew confirmed. "You're the first person we've ever told this to."

"Not even your families?" Jonah probed.

"No one," Matthew answered. "Apart from the kids, no one knows. It wouldn't be safe for anyone else to know. The look we shared today was the realization that this union puts you in a position where you need to know. If it ever gets discovered and we're not around, it's essential that you know how to protect Lias."

A chill ran up Jonah's spine, taking precedence over every other word that had been uttered.

"No one will ever lay a finger on any of my family," Jonah snarled through clenched teeth. In a matter of moments, he had acquired a family he'd always wanted, and now someone was trying to take it away from him. Unprecedented rage surged through him, refusing to let him accept such an injustice.

"I'm sorry for dropping this bombshell on your evening," Matthew said, attempting to quell the ire he saw in Jonah's eyes. "Lias loves you with all his heart. I hope this doesn't affect your plans with him."

Jonah's eyes narrowed and bored into Matthew's. "Nothing will ever make me not want to be with him. It's like finding out that Santa is real after years of believing it's not possible. Knowing he's even more special now just makes me want to hold him tighter tonight."

As Jonah spoke, he couldn't tell if he was being honest. *Does this change how I feel?* he thought to himself. He didn't have the answer. He knew he needed to talk to Lias, not Matthew, about this. *Maybe I already know how I feel. I still want to be in this family.*

Matthew stood and gestured for Jonah to do the same.

He held Jonah in a tight embrace, and whispered in his ear, "Welcome to the family, son. I love you."

Jonah wept into Matthew's shoulder, barely believing the words he'd so desperately wanted to hear from his father but never would. He felt the sincerity in Matthew's embrace and trembled in response. Matthew's hand came to rest on the back of Jonah's head, and he stayed in that embrace until his tears had run dry.

Jonah realized that no matter what he discussed with Lias, he would remain a part of this family forever.

"Let's go find your fiancé," Matthew said softly. Jonah nodded, and the two of them left in search of Lias.

FIVE

L**eading the way,** Matthew descended the winding staircase and into the parlor. Allowing Jonah some privacy, he excused himself to check on the whereabouts of the rest of his family. As soon as Jonah was alone, the overwhelming stress of his new knowledge began to dissipate. The parlor always brought him a sense of calm.

On the north wall, the first thing one sees upon entering the house is a full-service home bar. Black high-backed stools were tucked against a service island, facing a wall-to-wall wine hutch. Countless aged bottles of wine from around the globe filled the shelves, captivating Jonah's imagination. He loved to envision the stories behind each bottle's journey to the parlor. The sea-treading voyages that brought them to their final destination.

Gleaming crystal wine goblets hung from their polished stems above the island countertop, reflecting the sunlight that poured through the windows and onto the chilled Italian marble. The sweet scent of cherries and bourbon always lingered in the air, bringing Jonah back to his father who used to enjoy a single glass of bourbon after work. He felt the familiar sting of tears in his eyes and reminded himself that it was only the alcohol; it was not him. *Compose yourself.*

On the western wall of the parlor was a stunning cobblestone fireplace. Each stone was unique in size, color, or shape. Remnants of the stones where Samuel and Matthew first stood together, Jonah was in awe of the captivating story that was forever embedded in this hearth. Above the stones, a beautiful driftwood mantle completed the look.

The eastern half of the parlor was raised 12 inches higher than the western half. Long slabs of solid rosewood ran north to south, with a full-sized Steinway piano in the center. Purple velvet keypads covered the keys. Jonah loved to sit in the parlor and listen to Matthew or Eternity playing the piano. The music always brought him a sense of peace and his imagination ran wild, imagining the relationship each note had with the rest. Each scribbled note ran across the page, racing one another to the end.

Behind the piano was a giant black plush floor-length stage curtain. Those standing behind it looked as if they were ready to entertain the queen, especially at night. During the day, the curtains were pulled to reveal a bay window with a reading nook spacious enough for any adult. This was Jonah's private sanctuary in the house. He often snuck away to this spot to read with the sun warming his skin or to write under the last rays of daylight.

On the southern wall, adjacent to the front door, Samuel had painted a large tree that branched out to cover the entire wall. Metallic green, auburn, and clay paints made up the leaves. As the years passed, more family photos were hung in the branches.

Love blooms from this tree, Jonah thought. *Love blooms from this family. Everything, and everyone, created by the love Matthew and Samuel share.* Jonah was envious. He dreamed of loving Lias just as deeply, to create everything he so cherished in this house.

In the center of the parlor, Jonah sat on the leather sectional that faced the family tree. His eyes moved around the room, just as they had countless times before, taking in every inch of family, every ounce of delight, and every ray of happiness that resided in this single place.

None of it matters, Jonah thought. *This home is a testament to the greatness of this family. There is so much love within these walls, and Matthew had bent the rules of the world for the man he loved. There is no fear here, only loads of lessons to learn about how to love someone deeply.*

"You're ridiculous!" Eternity declared as she trailed Lias back into the parlor, interrupting Jonah's peaceful sanctuary.

Lias approached Jonah, ignoring his sister's irritated banter, and knelt in front of him. Instinctively, he grabbed Jonah's hand. "Are you okay?" Lias asked, his voice soft and full of concern.

"I'm fine," Jonah answered, reaching to tenderly stroke the side of Lias' cheek with his index and forefinger.

"Are we okay?" Lias asked, studying Jonah's face for the truth.

"We're great, love," Jonah assured him, then pulled Lias' face closer for a heartfelt kiss. The familiar affection confirmed for Lias that Jonah was indeed okay. While one could hide behind words, the truth was always found in the electricity shared between their lips touching.

"I'm glad you're okay," Eternity agreed, realizing the depth of the conversation the whole family knew was just dropped on Jonah. "Now can you please tell your future husband that he's an idiot?"

Jonah chuckled. "I'm not sure that's the best way to start off my engagement. What seems to be the problem?"

"He doesn't like any of the venue ideas that may be available at the last minute," Eternity complained.

"I like them all," Lias corrected, shooting his sister a menacing glare. "I just don't see the point in spending a lot of money for a ceremony. We can just do it at City Hall. Cheap, quick, easy, and done."

"Absolutely not!" Tavia joined in. "No brother of mine…"

Jonah zoned out of the conversation. He found the wedding banter hilarious. As an only child, he had never experienced siblings arguing about anything and found the whole thing absolutely entertaining. He was amazed to see how they could get so angry with one another and still come out of the conversation with their relationship unscathed.

"Children, please take a moment and breathe," Matthew's commanding voice left no room for debate. "While I'm sure everyone has the best intentions for this wedding, it is about two people—Lias and Jonah. It doesn't matter what any of us think they should do. This memory will be the first of their many steps together as one. We do not have the right to decide for them what that day should look like. Lias has made it clear what he thinks. Perhaps it is time to see if Jonah has any thoughts on the matter."

The room full of eyes shifting to meet his face created a familiar burning sensation in Jonah's cheeks. He could feel himself blushing under the scrutiny of so many. Jonah did not enjoy being in the spotlight.

"Whatever Lias wants to do is fine with me," Jonah said with a deflated breath.

Lias picked up on this immediately, turning his back to his sisters and taking both of Jonah's hands in his.

"I don't think we should start off this union with a lie, do you?" Lias asked.

"No," Jonah answered.

"I don't care where or how we get married," Lias said, holding onto Jonah's hands tightly. "All I care about is that it happens. I just don't see the point in spending a lot of money for one day. But this day is about you too, baby. What do you want us to do?"

"Well," Jonah said, his eyes wandering around the room. "I like the idea of having a special day full of beautiful pictures we can look at to remember. If I end up like Mom," he said quietly, "they may be all I have someday."

Jonah never spoke of the always looming, unspoken fear that he could end up like Vivian, unaware of those around him. At the mere mention of it, obvious waves of emotion rippled through Lias, making him stiffen.

"Then that is what we will do," Lias declared firmly. "Money can always be made."

For the first time, Samuel broke his silence. "We can always help with that."

Jonah's gaze landed on Lias as he asked, "What if we can have both? What if we have the wedding here in this room? A few decorations strung about. This room has always been a sanctuary for me, and I can't think of anywhere more perfect to start our life together than right here."

Lias glanced quickly at his fathers, who both nodded in agreement, before turning his gaze back to Jonah. "Then right here is where it will be." He kissed the top of Jonah's hand. "Let's keep it simple and compromise. Just family."

All eyes in the room landed on the young couple. "We only have a few weeks to put this together," Lias declared. "We're going to need everyone's help to make it perfect."

He pointed to Eternity. "Can you please oversee the music? Nothing too extravagant. Whatever you pick will be fine."

"Of course," she answered.

Jonah beamed. This was the man he loved, a natural decision-maker and compromiser. He was thrilled at how quickly things were coming together.

Lias then addressed Tavia. "It wouldn't be much of a wedding without a rehearsal dinner. Do you mind taking care of that? And the cake? You have complete autonomy."

"No doubt!" Tavia answered.

Lias turned to Samuel. "We'll need help finding and picking out suits. Can you help us?"

"I think I can manage that," Samuel chuckled, still wearing his three-piece suit from work.

"Papa," Lias choked out, his voice starting to break. "You designed this room. It would only make sense that you are the best suited to transform it into a wedding chapel. Do you mind?"

"I can think of nothing I would love to do more for the two of you," Matthew cheered.

Jonah asked, "What about me?"

Lias smiled at him. "You, my dear, have the most important job of all—making sure I stay calm for the next four weeks and do not sabotage our perfect day."

"Great! Something I have tons of practice in!" Jonah declared.

The room filled with laughter and quickening chatter as everyone started discussing their new assignments. Jonah watched in awe as the family came together in the familiar way he had seen them do a million times over the years: decide, then execute.

* * *

"Freshen that for you?" the overly helpful barmaid asked, pulling away Lias' drink before he had a chance to answer, no doubt trying to loosen his pockets to increase her tip. Lias was happy that all the events of the day had inspired Jonah to write while the inspiration was hot; it gave him an excuse to be alone, under the guise of being a supportive partner.

He nodded, moving his busy eyes around the room, taking in the near-empty bar. A few patrons were shooting pool, full of laughter at the obvious lack of skill between them. A lone couple was slowly swaying side to side in the darkest corner of the dance floor, to music that was way too up-tempo for their slow footwork. A few older patrons were enjoying the overpriced and under-flavored bar food.

The near solitude of this usually hopping place was a welcome change tonight. Lias was not here to party; he was here to reflect.

"I made it a double," the red-haired barmaid admitted as she set the sweating drink down in front of Lias. "It looks like you could use it. Rough day?"

"Not at all," Lias answered with facial expressions that did not quite match his words. "I got engaged today."

"Buyer's remorse already?" the busy-bodied bartender nervously wiped in an endless circle around the already clean bar.

"Ha! Please," Lias retorted. "Jonah is the best, and I've known most of my life that we would be married young."

"So why does your face not share that excitement now?" she pushed.

"Marrying Jonah is going to be great," Lias smiled, trying harder to show the truth behind that statement. "It's everything that comes after that worries me."

"Oh?" was all the prompting Lias needed to continue.

"Jonah is old-fashioned and committed; as soon as we get married, he'll be ready to find a house, plant a garden, get matching SUVs, start a family, and a 401K. Now don't get me wrong, all those things in time are obviously ideal. But I'm barely 21 and still like the idea of a studio flat apartment in Manhattan. I don't want to have to worry about mowing grass to keep up with the neighbors. I want to pass out on the rooftop of a skyscraper after painting the town red. I'm not ready to change diapers and be in bed by 9 p.m."

Lias took a heaping sip of his cocktail, replaying the words he had just admitted to the young tavern hand, as well as to himself.

"Sounds like a talk with him needs to happen before the wedding," the bartender held a finger up as she was called away to the other end of the bar for a new group of three placing their orders.

"No way," Lias spoke to the lifeless dishtowel left behind as the bartender whisked away.

Following the new group, a string of patrons began flooding in.

That will be my cue to cash out, Lias thought, and he held a finger up, pointing to the door to signal he was ready to go. *Maybe I can bridge the subject without being the bad guy. I could say that I don't want to set up roots until after graduate school. Jonah couldn't be upset about that, could he? We haven't discussed what the next phase of education for us will look like yet. Maybe it can be grad school in NYC.*

While Lias wasn't thrilled about the idea of further education, the idea of making a splash in the Big Apple before becoming a family man did sound appealing. Even if it meant he had to deal with a few more years of school. *That is a fair trade*, Lias concluded.

SIX

The weeks flew by like a thief in the night. Staring at his desk calendar, the page with the bright red circle around June 14 was edging closer and could easily be seen bleeding through the few pages that remained before it, as Lias crumpled up the page before tossing it into the wastebasket. He wiped the early morning sleep from his eyes, glancing back at Jonah who was still fast asleep.

I have a perfect life, Lias thought. *What more could I want?*

A loud, persistent pounding shook the apartment door. Over and over again. The silence between the knocks was getting shorter and shorter. Lias flung open the door to find five sharply dressed military police officers standing there.

"Nickelias Anderson?" the center MP asked.

"Yes, that's me," Lias answered in his state of confusion.

"You are going to have to come with us," another chimed in.

Two of the MPs made their way past Lias, toward the movement of Jonah who was now stumbling out of bed, at the sound of the ruckus. The two now in the apartment were lifting Jonah up, one on each arm, and a third spoke loud enough for both boys to hear.

"Nickelias Anderson and Jonah Greene, you are both being charged with aiding and abetting treason against the United States of America government."

Lias, having been trained in martial arts since his infancy, was mentally prepared to fight and run until he looked back at Jonah, stumbling to stay on his own feet. He could escape, but he would have to leave Jonah behind. Only days before their union, he was not prepared to do that. He would obey the commands of the MPs and look for an opportunity for them both to escape together.

"Wha—?" Jonah started to ask, but Lias quickly moved a finger to his lips, instructing Jonah to remain silent.

"It's okay, baby," Lias spoke in his softest voice. "Just do as they say."

Jonah nodded in understanding. His still sleep-filled state reminded him that he was in no position to refuse the clear instructions his partner had just given him. He would trust Lias' judgment now.

The boys, still in their pajamas, were escorted out of their home and into a waiting, solid black SUV that had a tint so dark that you could not see inside. The boys were wedged between two MPs, one against each door. The two were not cuffed, but the weapons at each MPs waist gave them enough authority that Lias was not about to risk making a move that could harm Jonah in the crossfire of his impulsive action. The other two men piled into the front of the SUV, and it started to move.

"Where are you taking us?" Jonah asked.

"Shut up, traitor. No questions," the driver snapped, staring at the pair through the rearview mirror.

Lias reached for Jonah's hand. Without a word, he let him know that they were in this together. Wherever the SUV took them, they would figure it out together. Jonah squirmed, obviously preparing for some type of action. Lias tightened his grip to relax his fiancé.

"It will be okay," Lias whispered. "Stay calm."

Staying calm was an impossible ask, but Jonah knew Lias had been trained from a baby to take care of himself. So, he stopped squirming.

This must be the exact scenario that Matthew fears for kids, Jonah thought. *This is what he warned me about. This is why his kids were all experts in martial arts. If I can just get the chance to draw their attention, then Lias can easily escape.* Jonah traced every inch of the car with his eyes, looking for anything he could use for a distraction. Moving as slowly as he could, not to draw attention to what he was doing. His scanning stopped when he got to the face of his fiancé.

Jonah stared at Lias, wondering what he was thinking. What he was planning. Jonah knew all too well that there was no way Lias entered this car so calmly without a plan. His words must be some type of clue. Jonah mulled them over again and again in silence, looking for the clue.

Lias was attentive but had no plan in place that would save the two of them. And Lias was not about to execute any plan that would separate them or potentially harm Jonah. Not even if it put his own life in danger.

"We have the right to an attorney if we are being detained," Jonah challenged confidently.

"You have the right to shut up," the irritated driver snapped back. "Where you are going, not even the best lawyer can help you."

The MPs shared an agreeing look before remaining silent.

They drove west out of the city, and Lias kept a sharp eye out for any clues as to their destination. As they reached the state line to Alabama, they turned between two desolate fields. The SUV slowed and eventually came to a stop. Ahead, Lias could see a helicopter waiting with two pilots outside, helmets on and ready to fly.

Still outnumbered, Lias and Jonah followed their captors' directions to exit the car and walk toward the SUV. One of the men reached back into the SUV and pulled out a stuffed duffle bag. Lias was certain there was a supply of weapons inside. If only he could find a moment to break away without Jonah being harmed, the weapons in the bag would be enough for them to escape.

Jonah eyed the distance between the SUV and the helicopter. His chances of making a successful run for it were quickly disappearing. The MPs were trained well—whenever Jonah adjusted his course, one of them would flank him back on the direct course to the helicopter. His chance to run and save himself had passed. Jonah sighed, resigned. The MP handling the duffle bag passed it off to the shorter of the two pilots. Once they were in the air, Lias knew their opportunities for escape would be nonexistent. He needed to stall long enough for a window to present itself. If they boarded that helicopter, their fates would be sealed. He had to buy more time.

"Listen," Lias addressed the pilots. "I don't know what orders you have or what you think holding us hostage will do for the safety of the country, but we are not a threat to anyone."

"I am not acting on anyone's orders," the shorter pilot holding the duffle answered in a strangely familiar voice.

"Then why are you doing this?" Lias asked, trying to place the husky voice underneath the white helmet.

"I was given no orders, so I made my own," the bag-holding pilot confirmed, dropping the duffle to the ground.

Lias and Jonah slowly stepped forward, knowing that if they stopped, the MPs behind them would start shooting.

"What orders have you given yourself?" Lias asked as he watched the pilot unbuckle the strap of his helmet.

"I have ordered myself to make sure this is a day you two never forget," the pilot answered with a sinister chuckle, as he removed his helmet.

Lias and Jonah stopped in their tracks. Jonah glanced at Lias, then turned again to face the pilot, whose face was the same as his fiancée's, only this one wore a sinister smile, while Lias' face was etched with anger.

"Since I was given no assignment," the pilot wearing Lias' face said, "I put myself in charge of the bachelor's party."

"You motherfucker," Lias yelled, now running towards his twin brother with Jonah in tow. "Do you have any idea what you just put us through?"

As they closed the gap toward his brother, the SUV could be heard driving away, leaving only the four of them alone in the field.

"My bet is something you will never forget," Matswell answered.

"Where did you get those guys from? And where did you get a helicopter?" Lias asked, punching his brother before reaching in for a tear-filled hug.

"That would be all me," the other pilot—a feminine voice—said behind him, as she removed her helmet.

"Tavia, you asshole," Lias screamed, "you were in on this?"

"Well, what did you expect?" Tavia asked. "You gave me the rehearsal dinner party, and no one the real party. So, when Matswell called back and found out he had been given nothing to do, we decided to remedy that ourselves."

"He was assigned nothing to do," Lias barked. "The asshole didn't answer his phone or bother calling me back for the last three weeks."

"To be fair," Matswell replied, "I did call back. Tavia answered. I thought this would be more memorable this way."

"Jerks," Jonah mumbled. "I think I crapped myself in the car. Five minutes after learning the family secret, I'm dragged off by military police."

Still trying to convince himself there was no longer a reason to run, Jonah turned his back to his new family and took in a deep, calming breath. He now had his first taste of what it was like to have siblings. His role now was crystal clear: forgive, and move forward. It was all done out of the best intentions, even if they may not have seemed that way.

"We're sorry," Tavia apologized, placing a single hand on Jonah's shoulder. "We were just going to grab Lias, but—"

"But," Matswell added, "I reminded her that it's your bachelor party too."

SEVEN

The chaotic whirlwind of the last twenty-four hours still spun in Jonah's head as he walked through the wrought iron gate, up the hedgerow-lined driveway to Anderson Manor, the nickname Matthew had given to their home. Jonah worried that even after two showers, the smell of alcohol and fraternity brotherhood may still linger on his body. The tender skin on his shoulder throbbed from the impulsive tattoo he had allowed himself to get while high on adrenaline. The word

Reveuse was now a permanent reminder for him of what he held most important in life.

Would they notice anything? Jonah wondered. *Would they say anything if they did?*

Stealing a glance at Lias, he knew they would notice, and they would not say a word. He could remember dozens of times Lias had been caught sneaking up this same walkway with Matswell and him in tow from whatever wild night Lias had dragged them both on. Matswell never wanted to go any more than Jonah did, but saying no to Lias was not an option.

Lias had a way about him that you knew whatever he was getting into should be avoided at all costs, yet you wanted to do it anyway. Just to see what he would do next. His parents knew how to manage him. While most parents would scold and forbid such behaviors, all but ensuring their children would repeat or even escalate their antics, Matthew and Samuel always acknowledged it and then went out of their way to appear unfazed by his misadventures.

They would then give him whatever punishment they deemed appropriate. These dads viewed punishment as a form of currency—every action outside of the house rules had a price to be paid with their chosen currency.

At younger ages, the price was often a certain amount of time out or giving up a prized toy for a set duration. As the children got older, they had to forfeit their phones, do extra chores, or complete community service. Sometimes allowances were withheld and other times they had to pay back or work off monetary fines.

Jonah understood this system as practice for the real world. In the same way that laws have to be followed or fines enforced by courts in a city, state, or country, living in this house meant Samuel and Matthew set the cost of each action. The more undesirable the offense, the higher the cost—and repeated offenses had an escalating price, usually making it not worth the effort.

Visitors, even Jonah, were subject to the same set of house rules while at the manor. Breaking any one of these rules would result in a similar fine, and continual violation of the rules would mean being unable to return. It seemed odd to Jonah, who was raised with this family, that children were allowed to be so free—provided they were willing to pay the consequences.

In contrast, Jonah, when first exposed to this strange system, noticed tension in the homes of his grade school classmates, with a perpetual power struggle and hatred. His new siblings, however, were all well-versed in the concept that every action has a price. The conversation he always heard in the Anderson home was not one of asking permission, but rather "What will doing this cost me?"

As they reached the front door, Samuel opened it before either boy could reach for the handle. Samuel was impeccably dressed, making the expensive suits the boys wore appear to be mere toys. Samuel's formal attire was a specialty of his, and he knew how to make even the most mundane cloth shine like a star in the night sky. Jonah couldn't help but feel underdressed.

As they stepped into the house, Chopin filled the air as Matthew sat at the Steinway. Jonah hadn't memorized the name of the piece, but he had heard it enough before to recognize the composer. The music brought a smile to his face.

The boys were completely in the dark as to what Tavia had in store for the rehearsal dinner. She had been given absolute freedom in making her selections, but after her recent abduction of them, Jonah began to question whether Lias had made the best decision by granting her such a large amount of power.

Lias had wanted to forgo the whole idea of a rehearsal dinner, but Jonah was adamant that all the classic elements of a wedding should be present. With the agreement that only the immediate family would be in attendance, both were willing to accept the compromise.

The aromas emanating from the kitchen were unmistakable, yet Jonah couldn't quite put his finger on what they were. He glanced around the room, observing the family all dressed to the nines, and the scents seemed incongruous with the attire. Lias tried to sneak a look, but Tavia quickly ushered him to take a seat at the table.

Just as the boys were seated, the front door burst open with boisterous voices. It was Eternity who had arrived, proclaiming to Vivian not to be concerned with the dirt on her feet and to come inside.

Jonah jumped up from his chair. He had not even thought to invite his mother to the event. He felt a wave of remorse, realizing that he had not included her. He was grateful to have a sister-in-law who was aware of the situation and acted accordingly.

"I'd gone to Vivian's home to see if she had any baby pictures," Eternity explained. "Imagine my surprise when I found her still in her room and not on the way here. So, I took advantage of my authority over the charge nurse and checked her out for a few hours."

"Hi Mom," Jonah said, stumbling forward to greet her. "Let me help you."

"Thank you," Vivian replied, taking in his formal attire. "Getting married, are we?"

"It seems so, if all goes according to plan," Jonah said, a wide smile spreading across his face.

Jonah guided her to a chair next to his at the lengthy table. The sun had already begun to set, so he knew better than to hope that she would remember who anyone was or why they were all gathered there. Still, he was pleased to have her with them. It felt more real now, more complete. He would have to thank Eternity later in private for this moment.

Vivian stayed quiet. Matthew rose from the piano and Eternity sat down in his place. She switched to a slower, more tranquil melody, noticing how entranced Vivian was with the music.

"Dinner should be interesting," Matthew commented as he excused himself to see what Tavia was up to.

"What does that mean, Dad?" Lias asked, directing his gaze to Samuel.

"I'd rather let her show you the surprise herself," Samuel replied. "I'd hate to have the military police knocking on my door tomorrow." Matthew gave Lias a knowing look. Just then, the kitchen door swung open, and Tavia backed through it carrying a huge tray of miniature burger sliders in one hand, and a second tray of crinkled French fries in the other. She quietly placed them in the center of the table before retreating to the kitchen. Lias stared at the food and then at his father in confusion.

"She felt the best rehearsal dinner for *your* wedding would be one that served your favorite food," Samuel explained.

Lias felt a spark of joy inside of him at the sight of his father dressed as the world's fanciest waiter, setting down two trays of burgers from the cheapest drive-thru in town. The spark grew until he found himself laughing at the absurdity of the situation.

Jonah looked at him in bewilderment, as if to ask, *Is everything all right?*

"It's perfect," Lias answered between fits of laughter. "It's exactly right."

"I didn't forget about you Jonah," Tavia said as she brought out the next two platters stacked to the max with individually wrapped tacos.

"Why did you get him tacos? Those aren't his favorite," Lias questioned.

"They are according to his bank statement for the last six months," Tavia answered.

Lias quickly turned to face Jonah, not at all shocked that his sister had done something so outrageous, but to confirm if she was right.

"They are my guilty pleasure," Jonah admitted. Although he was definitely offended at the invasion of his privacy, he chose to let it be for the night and instead focused on the mountain of tacos that were now in front of him.

"Don't start yet," Tavia commanded as she and Matthew darted back into the kitchen.

The front door opened and Matswell rushed in, bags in each hand. His bow tie hung untied around his neck, and his jacket was slung over his arm as he hastened to join the family at the table.

"Sorry I'm late," he apologized.

"Let me take those," Samuel offered, retrieving the bags and motioning Matswell toward the washroom to freshen up before dinner.

When Matswell returned, the table was fully set. In addition to the sliders, fries, and tacos, there were now a variety of salsas, onion ring cheesecakes, and German chocolate cake, all served on the family's finest china.

"As a doctor, I must advise against partaking in this meal," Eternity cautioned.

"Your objection is noted," Lias replied, his eyes fixed hungrily on the towering burgers.

"Leave it to our family to have such an eclectic arrangement of foods to celebrate the first wedding in this generation," Matthew said, his face beaming with pride.

"Leave it to Lias to be the youngest, but the first to marry," Eternity added.

"Youngest by minutes," Lias corrected.

"My baby all the same," Samuel said warmly.

By that point, the whole family was seated and waiting for a signal to start. Just then, Tavia stood up.

"I just want to say," she began, her voice hoarse, "I could not be more delighted at my little brother's choice for a life partner." She shifted her gaze from Lias to Jonah. "I've thought of you as another annoying little brother for years now. After tomorrow, I guess that will be set in stone. Only I get to torment my little brothers.

If you don't treat him right, a mob of MPs at your door will be the least of your worries."

Jonah nodded, accepting the clear warning.

"Who's getting married?" Vivian asked, only now noticing all the finely dressed people in the room.

"We are, Momma," Jonah answered, holding up their intertwined hands.

"Oh," Vivian said, her expression softening. "How did you two boys meet?"

"If you don't mind," Eternity interjected, already standing up. The couple nodded, giving her permission to share the story.

"I had just turned 21, the same age lias is now" Eternity began. "I was home for the summer from college, trying to earn some extra money for the upcoming semester for a few guilty pleasures. I distributed some flyers offering private piano lessons for the summer. After a few days, I got a call from the sweetest woman." She smiled fondly at Vivian.

"She told me she was in a bind with her son and asked if I would be willing to babysit him after school for a few hours, at the rate I was advertising for music lessons. She thought that if I had the patience to teach piano to small children, I'd be well-suited to look after her nearly-mute, introverted 11-year-old. Though some parents leave their kids home alone these days, his father's passing made her worry too much to do the same." Vivian's eyes glistened as she soaked in the story.

"I wanted the money," Eternity admitted. "It worked out perfectly for me since I wouldn't have to find multiple students. I could earn the same money watching one charming little boy. I was already watching two brothers of the same age for free anyway." The family chuckled in agreement.

"I did try to teach him the piano at first," Eternity continued. "But it was immediately clear that was a lost cause. The only thing in the house that interested him was my brother, Lias. They clicked instantly. It was a connection they both desperately needed. When I put up the flyer, I was looking for a student. Instead, I ended up with a brother. I couldn't be happier."

"Here, here!" The family cheered in unison, their glasses clinking together as laughter filled the room. Jonah's eyes brimmed with tears, threatening to spill over.

EIGHT

The **incessant** pounding of the jackhammer outside his thin-walled apartment jolted Jonah awake. He reached to kiss Lias, but instead of finding warm lips, his hand met a familiar, well-worn pillow. He remembered last night, when his mother Vivian had reminded him, even though she couldn't recall who he was, not to see the groom before the wedding. Despite the fact that she wouldn't ever know, Jonah and Lias had both agreed to honor the request, so Lias had returned to his old room, and taco-filled Jonah had been sent home to his own bed.

Today was finally here. Every follicle on Jonah's body tingled with excitement. It would be the last night he would ever go to sleep without being married to Lias—a dream he'd been fantasizing about for years. He had been given strict instructions not to show up at the house until 5 p.m., leaving him with an entire day to fill. Getting ready wouldn't take long.

His soon-to-be sisters-in-law had taken Vivian out for a morning of pampering to get ready for the wedding, but Jonah hadn't been invited. Eternity teased him when he'd tried to join, her words still ringing in his ears: "Girls only!" He couldn't use that as a way to pass the time.

Most grooms and brides were filled with stress on the Big Day, but Jonah's new family had taken the burden off of them, something he would always be grateful for. Lias didn't handle large amounts of stress well and, even though their wedding was quite intimate, it could have easily sent him into a tailspin.

With hours to spare and nothing left to do, Jonah decided to spend a bit of his wedding day with the only family he had who wouldn't be at the ceremony. He splashed some water on his face, threw on a pair of jeans, a t-shirt, and a ball cap, then set out.

The lush green grass rustled beneath his sandals as Jonah walked the familiar path. His feet remembered every twist and turn of the boundless maze. The remnants of a foggy breeze lingered in the morning air as he reached his permanently saved seat on the ground.

"Well," Jonah spoke, clearing the groggy phlegm from his throat. "I'm getting married today. I know. Who would have thought, right? Lias is amazing—such a perfect balance for me. Between you and me though, Tavia can be a bit scary. You won't tell, will you?" He placed his palm against the cold black marble stone.

"I'll take that as a no," Jonah answered himself. "I don't want you to worry about me. It's been a rough few years without you, but after today I'll have two more dads looking out for me. They can never replace you, obviously, but they do love me. I hope that's all right with you. I miss you every day and I hope I make you proud."

Jonah sat by his dad's grave, scribbling into his overly worn leather-bound journal. It had been a while since he'd done this, usually a weekly occurrence, but with all the excitement since classes had let out for the summer, his visits had been put on the back burner.

The morning sun hung high above the green mounds, glaring brightly, trying to coax Jonah to surrender and turn back. With squinted eyes, and the faint laughter he heard echoing in the wind, it was easier for him to imagine the children playing in the grassy knoll across the cobbled street. But when he scanned the area, it was only his wild imagination. Jonah wrote their story as he imagined it.

The morning dew glistens upon the verdant landscape as I behold with admiration the spectacle of youth in a game of tag—a generational favorite that still brings out the childhood innocence in us all. Lilly, the sweet urchin, sprints away with a fleetness that belies her tender years, her flaming tresses streaming behind her as she eludes her freckled brother Ashton with all the vigor of a hunted deer. With a determined grin, Ashton pursues, galloping with all the energy of a lion. As the two collide, an explosion of jubilation ensues, and it is clear that it is time for the repast that has been laid out for them. I smile as I watch the pair hasten to the red and black checkered blanket, where their father waits with open arms and a feast of delights.

Jonah continued writing, imagining this family across the way until the sun's rays dried the last of the morning dew. He wrote until the book's final pages were filled, unable to contain even one more word.

The hours were quickly passing, and Jonah's window of free time was closing. As he rose to leave, Jonah reached to clear away some debris that had collected atop his father's tombstone.

"Ouch," he muttered, as something from the pile pricked his thumb. Drops of blood emerged, and he instinctively sucked them away until they stopped. "See you later Dad," he said, turning and heading back up the street to where his morning had begun.

Dust flew as Jonah opened the rusty garage door to his storage unit. Inside, he had stored sentimental items too large for their apartment, waiting for the day they could have a bigger place. Squeezing through a narrow but concealed path, he slithered like a snake through the obstacle course. Out of sight, tucked under a hand-me-down tapestry in the corner, Jonah observed the full three-shelf bookcase.

Journals filled the shelves, each one filled with the mindless ramblings of a young man struggling to find his way. Writing was Jonah's personal therapy, his own secret way of adjusting to the world. No one, not even Lias, knew of the journals he kept. While Lias was away, Jonah continued to write, though he never shared his story, the story of his life, with anyone.

Jonah's hand clasped a leather-bound book, which he had taken with him to see his father that morning. He carefully placed it on the third shelf, all the way against the edge. As he was walking away, he noticed his thumb had started to bleed again. Now, a red thumbprint was visible on the rough leather cover.

Perhaps it's fitting that the bookcase is full now, Jonah thought. After all, today is the last day of my life as a single man; the next bookcase will contain the entries of a married man. A smile spread across Jonah's face at the thought.

NINE

Lias stared at the reflection of the over-dressed man in the mirror. Today, he woke up feeling like a teenager, but the man looking back at him was far from that. His tall, wavy hair stood confidently, ready for the day. He thought about shaving, but the natural stubble was too iconic to change.

His slim-cut orange vest hung picturesquely over the perfectly pressed white shirt, with two black buttons below his ginger bow tie. The form-fitting black trousers made the creamy orange of his vest pop. Lias was grateful that Samuel had taken care of the wedding wardrobe. This was a moment he would relish proudly over and over again.

How much longer do I have to stay here? Lias wondered, fiddling with his already-perfect bow tie for the hundredth time.

Meanwhile, Lias wondered what Jonah was doing today all alone. Someone—Tavia he assumed—had snuck in and swiped his cell phone while he was sleeping. It was a very military move. "Disable communication, check," he could imagine it written on a clipboard checklist she was working from. The image was interrupted by a knock at the door.

Finally, someone has come to free me, Lias thought.

"Knock, knock," Samuel announced as he closed the door behind himself. "You look very dapper."

"Thank you," Lias smiled. "Have you come to rescue me?" he asked.

"Not quite," Samuel answered. "I don't think your sisters, or your Papa, are ready for you yet. I was actually hoping that you and I could have a conversation before everything."

"Of course, Dad," Lias answered. "What's going on?"

"Well," Samuel said, looking towards the floor.

"That bad?" Lias asked.

"No, no baby," Samuel raised his eyes to meet his questioning son. "It's nothing bad, just a big day for a dad. You're my first child to get married. You're still my baby."

"Come sit down and talk to me, Dad," Lias said, motioning to the small table in Matthew's study. He took a seat on one side, his expression a mix of apprehension and excitement.

"As I was saying, you're my first baby to get married. I'm not sure what's, you know, acceptable or not," Samuel said as he settled into the chair opposite his son. "We've never been big on trying to force anything on you or your siblings."

"I know, and I've always appreciated that," Lias said, a hint of a smile tugging at the corners of his lips. "So, what are you trying to 'force' on me today?"

Samuel returned his son's smile. "I wouldn't say 'force'. I just want to push a little bit on something, if you'll indulge me."

Lias nodded.

"Growing up the way I did, I never quite understood how I fit into a lot of the boxes other people so easily slid into," Samuel began. "I knew I was different, and I'm still trying to figure out where I stand sometimes. I know you've decided you don't need rings, but I'd like to point out that while being your own person is almost always the best choice, there are times when tradition can add more value than you can imagine."

He paused to gauge his son's reaction, not expecting the quiet, inquisitive eyes that greeted him.

"Symbols have power," Samuel continued. "Wedding rings have the power to show the depth of love and devotion you have for another person. They tell the world you're spoken for, that you have a place to belong. But more than anything, they tell your partner that everywhere you go, you are sending that message with the ring on your finger.

"I know Jonah would do anything to make you happy," he continued, "and I think it would make him very happy if you were sending out that message. To many men, including him, that kind of gesture is invaluable. It's a very powerful thing."

"You really think wearing a piece of metal on my finger would mean that much to him?" Lias asked, incredulous.

"I do," Samuel answered. "But I don't think he'd want you to know just how much it would mean to him if it doesn't mean as much to you."

Samuel's hands fidgeted in his pockets.

"You bought rings, didn't you?" Lias asked. "Where are they? Let me see them."

"I may have," Samuel admitted. "I don't want to force you into anything. I just want to give you the option. I'll put them on the table, and if you decide to use them in the ceremony, great. If not, that's great too. Today is all about you."

"And Jonah," Lias corrected, his gaze traveling to the two unopened boxes his father had just placed next to him.

"And Jonah," Samuel repeated, his hand already on the doorknob.

"Thank you, Dad," Lias said before his father closed the door.

He picked up the first box, feeling its weight in the palm of his hand. Flipping open the lid, he saw an engraving that read 'something old and borrowed.' Inside was a pair of Samuel's iconic charcoal-colored cufflinks.

So traditional, Dad, Lias thought, reflecting on Vivian's idea of tradition that had stayed with her even as she was beginning to lose herself. His father's message of tradition also echoed in his mind. They had such a strong relationship. Lias began to wonder if he too should embrace tradition more. After all, he wanted his marriage to Jonah to be just as strong as his own parents' had been.

He opened the second box, revealing two almost identical wedding bands. The inscription on the lid read 'New and Blue.' The rings were polished silver on the inside and around the edges, while a sea-blue band wrapped around the flat top. A gemstone was embedded at the front of each ring, above the message 'Forever.'

"Am I interrupting?" a soft voice asked. Lias looked up to see Matthew, observing him spinning one of the rings in his hand. He had been so absorbed in the rings that he hadn't even noticed his father's approach.

"I believe you and I have a walk to take soon," Matthew said.

Lias rose to his feet and pocketed one of the rings, handing the other to his father. Matthew nodded in acknowledgment that he was to give it to Jonah.

"Finally," Lias said with a grin.

"Don't rush today, son," Matthew advised. "It will be over in a flash, and you'll think about today more often than you realize."

Lias stepped out onto the top of the winding staircase and was met with the sound of beautiful music. Eternity was playing a composition that felt both familiar and new. From the top, Lias could see that the room had been completely transformed overnight. The stairs were lined with fresh green ivy, while Georgia magnolias and their vibrant orange, red, and brown leaves blanketed the path down the steps, up the aisle to where Jonah stood, beaming.

The family tree on the northern wall was adorned with pictures of Jonah and Lias. A wooden arch stood in front of the fireplace, wrapped in ivy and honeysuckle, from which a sweet scent wafted up the stairs. The glasses that usually hang above the home bar had been replaced with silver crystal wind chimes.

Lias felt his eyes fill with tears as he realized his family had recreated the scene of Jonah's proposal. Every detail had been painstakingly replicated.

Jonah stood beneath the arch wearing an orange suit jacket, white shirt, and black tie. His eyes met Lias', silently begging him to come closer. As Lias began to take the first step down the staircase, Eternity's music shifted, and Tavia started singing. The petals crunched softly beneath his feet.

Tavia's voice filled the room with its majestic beauty, each word ringing its truth before she moved on to the next. They hadn't discussed the music, and Lias paused to take it all in before continuing down the stairs to join his beloved.

The familiar yet transformed words tightened around Lias' throat as he imagined singing along while frozen in place. Tavia nodded encouragingly to her baby brother, and Lias inhaled a lungful of the sweet air around him before mustering his courage and stepping forward.

With her voice vibrating in the background, Lias descended the staircase, Matthew escorting him with each step closer to the honey-scented altar. When he finally reached the bottom of the stairs, he felt as though Tavia had been guiding him the whole way.

Matthew smiled at his son then Jonah, before stepping away to the side. Lias extended his hand, and as if they had rehearsed it a million times, Tavia sang the next phrase on beat as their hands joined as one. The words faded away, leaving only a few bars of music from Eternity to play softly in the silence.

Matswell stood opposite Jonah, just outside the arch. His sisters stood beside Vivian. Together they created a picture of a family united.

Wow, this is really happening, Lias thought.

The scent of the room flooded Lias with memories, causing him to become lost in his own mind. Jonah's grip tightened, and he began to speak.

"When I was a young gay boy, struggling to find where I fit in the world, I felt lost," Jonah said sweetly. "Then, by chance, we found each other, and you saved me. You gave me a purpose in a time when I had none. After my dad passed away, I started to spiral. You held onto me and saved me once more. When my mother started getting lost in herself, I was done. I was slipping away, and you kept me, you saved me. Now, because of you, I have a family larger than I could have ever dreamed of. I love you, Lias. Today I commit to no longer needing saving. I pledge to you in front of our family that I will spend the rest of our lives together, saving you."

Jonah retrieved the ring from his pocket and slid it onto Lias' finger.

Dad was right, Lias thought. He was glad he had trusted his father's wisdom. The look of satisfaction on Jonah's face was breathtaking.

"Jonah," Lias cleared his throat. "It was in this very room when I first laid eyes on you. I knew immediately that I wanted to be close to you. As a young child, I had no idea what that meant. But like all children, I knew it was important to get what I wanted. Growing beside you has been and will continue to be the most rewarding thing I have ever experienced. I may doubt and question things about the world around me, but I will never question you. There is no one better suited to deal with my crazy than you."

The family laughed as Lias placed a beautiful, shining ring on Jonah's finger. The sun's last beams illuminated the boys' faces as they kissed, sealing their commitment. The room filled again with sweet music.

"Presenting to you for the very first time," Tavia proclaimed, "Mr. and Mr. Jonah Greene."

TEN

Laughter filled the dining room as the family gathered together to enjoy this traditional meal. Sitting beside his husband, Lias felt absolute contentment as he looked around the room and saw the joy on his family's faces.

Matswell tapped his spoon against his glass, clearing his throat to get everyone's attention. "Growing up as a twin, you learn early on that every experience is a shared experience. You learn to walk alike, talk alike, and dress alike. Even when you are trying to be unique, the sense of individuality is more difficult than it is for those without a twin. Today is especially hard for me because, although I am very happy for the two of you, it marks the day that I must start being my own person. Jonah, you better treat him well, or else I'll be more than happy to swoop in and take my other half back."

The giddy family raised their glasses in agreement, and the room was filled with the sound of clinking glasses as the toast was made.

Eternity then drifted back to the piano, nodding for her sister to join her. As Lias and Jonah stepped out onto the open floor in the parlor, ready for their first dance as a married couple, Tavia began to sing, filling the room with beautiful, soul-igniting words. Jonah held Lias close, his heart burning with passion and a yearning for an even deeper connection.

As they swayed to the music, their vows burned in their souls, reminding them of the light that they had found in one another. The couple danced without exchanging words, letting their emotions speak for them. Tavia's voice echoed in the room, the words and promises they had made to one another lingering in the air, accompanied by the sweet honey scent.

After their dance was over and they shared a sweet passionate kiss, Jonah joined Vivian. The two stared at Eternity, bringing the page of music written before her to life around them. Taking advantage of the moment, Lias quietly slipped out the back door and settled on the porch. He welcomed the peacefulness that surrounded him, allowing him to take a few moments of respite.

Just then, the sound of his father's voice broke his reverie. "Who would have thought my youngest child would be the first to get married?" Matthew asked.

"—by only a few minutes," Lias qualified.

"Youngest still," Matthew echoed.

"You have been quite quiet since our engagement, Papa," Lias said. "What is on your mind tonight?"

"Well," Matthew began, "I am extremely proud. I know how hard it can be to have the courage to act on one's feelings at such a young age. To see the family growing organically like this is a father's dream. What are the next steps for the two of you?"

"We still plan to get down to the beach. A beach honeymoon seems appropriate," Lias answered.

"I wanted to talk to you about that," Matthew said, pulling an envelope out of his pocket. "I know I should have asked, but I wanted to give you a wedding gift. Inside this envelope is airfare, hotel, and food for an all-inclusive honeymoon."

Lias opened the envelope to find the destination. "Saint Barthelemy," he read. "Are you serious, Papa? You remembered?"

Matthew chuckled. "A father never forgets an obsession like that."

Lias stumbled up from his seat to give his father an adoring hug. Ever since he was a child, Lias had been obsessed with Saint Barts. After returning to their seats, the two sat together in silence, listening to the sounds of the Georgia night. It was a routine they had shared many times before and one of their favorite ways to converse. This very porch was the setting for many of these silent talks.

"There you are," Tavia announced as she pulled up a chair between them. "I wondered where you had escaped to."

"I have to know," Lias addressed his sister. "How did you manage to secure a military helicopter for a bachelor party kidnapping?"

Matthew shot his daughter a glance, obviously surprised by the news.

"Well," she answered. "We didn't exactly ask. My team refused to give up on why it went missing for 24 hours. As a result, we are all assigned to parks and recreation duty for 6 months. We will be checking old men for their hunting and fishing permits until New Year's, but it was totally worth it."

Matthew shook his head, piecing together the scenario in his mind that he was, for good reason, left in the dark about.

"You almost gave Jonah a heart attack," Lias shared. "Those guys are lucky that he was with me. Otherwise, there's no way I would have gone down without a fight."

"Matswell knew that," Tavia confessed. "That is why we planned to pick the two of you up together. I thought you would have fought anyway; that's what I would have done. But he was certain that if we kept Jonah seeming to be in danger, you would come along peacefully. It turns out he knows you better than I do. I now owe him $20. Thanks for that by the way."

"Thanks for betting that I would be selfish," Lias stuck his tongue out as he kicked his foot in the air in her direction in only the way a sibling could relate.

"Well, do me a favor brother," Tavia requested. "The next time you are confronted with men threatening to arrest you, please fight them. For my bank account's sake."

Even though he clearly disapproved of what happened, Matthew joined them in laughing at that request.

ELEVEN

Lias grumbled in protest as Jonah threw open the curtains, allowing a flood of morning light to stream into their corner hotel room. His eyes fought against the urge to open, and he added a super soft pillow to his face in an attempt to win the battle. But Jonah had an unfair advantage—he opened the window, and the swishing of the salt-filled waves crashing against the sand filled the suite. The scent of centuries-old salt drifted in the breeze, along with the joyous laughter of children playing on the beach. How could he possibly resist?

Despite wanting to rest from the long day before their trip, Lias knew that Jonah would not miss a single second of the adventure that had already taken over their honeymoon suite. This was something Lias had wanted to do since childhood, and Matthew had seen an opportunity to give a gift with double meaning and taken full advantage.

"Wake up, my love," Jonah teased, hovering over him, peppering his back with kisses.

"Let me sleep and you can do anything you want to me," Lias offered.

"As fun as you make that sound, I prefer to do anything I want to you while you're still awake," Jonah countered.

"Well then, let me sleep, and don't do anything to me," Lias joked, tightening the grip of the pillow around his head.

"Okay then, my love. You sleep. The bellboy was smiling at me last night when we checked in; maybe he wants to go for a walk on the beach with me," Jonah said.

Lias hurled the pillow at his teasing lover. Even though he knew Jonah was kidding, the thought of another man trying to seduce his husband was more than he could bear. The thought of the word 'husband' brought a huge smile to his face, and he rolled over onto his back, surrendering to the day.

"Well now that you're up..." Jonah teased, leaning in for a kiss.

"Nope," Lias retorted. "You had your chance, you were a prude about it, and that moment has passed."

The boys laughed together.

* * *

After polishing off a hearty breakfast, Lias' spirits began to lift for the day. As was no secret to those close to him, food always had a way of brightening his mood. His high metabolism was a blessing, allowing him to indulge in his love of food without consequence.

"What do you feel like doing today?" Jonah asked as soon as Lias popped the last bite of a cream-covered bagel into his mouth. "Is there something calling to you?"

Lias swallowed the bagel, seeds tumbling down his face and onto the floor, before taking a long swig of orange juice. "Hm, I was thinking of taking a bit of a stroll around the island," he replied. "Just to get to know the land a bit better."

"That sounds fun," Jonah grinned. "I heard from the staff that there are Jungle Jeep tours that leave every two hours down the beach."

"The staff?" Lias prodded, raising one eyebrow. "Or that scruffy bellhop?"

"The sweet girl at the check-in desk, if you must know," Jonah corrected, waving across the room at her as she was on the phone. "She told me the bellhop works the afternoon shift."

Jonah leaned across the table to give his pretend-jealous husband a kiss. The act of jealousy was a game they played out of habit, mocking couples they observed in person or on television. Despite the theatrics, both boys knew that there was nothing to be concerned about in their relationship. At this young point in their life, they have almost been together as many years as they had been apart.

After breakfast, the two strolled down to the beach. Jonah walked barefoot, the warm, soothing waves splashing against his ankles, while his feet sank into the wet sand with each step. Lias held his hand as they ambled along. The morning sun was warm, yet not oppressive. The beach was beautiful, with families scattered throughout, but not overly crowded. Just as Lias had always imagined it would be.

Lias stared into Jonah's profile as they walked, a look of contentment on his face that was hard to decipher. Jonah wasn't one for small talk, preferring to give his thoughts in few but powerful words. Nonetheless, Lias was used to reading the silent moments, and he could tell by the way Jonah was gripping his hand that he was exactly where he wanted to be. That kind of tight grip was only necessary when the stakes were high.

The peaceful saunter gave Lias a moment to reflect on the fact that he was married. He had always imagined it, but actually doing it was something entirely different. His thoughts drifted down a path of "what ifs," causing him to lose track of time until Jonah's deep voice brought his attention back to the present.

"Two please," Jonah said, handing his debit card to the old, tan-skinned man in a straw hat. "We would like the full tour with the lunch package."

"It'll be about thirty minutes," the old man replied, handing Jonah two tickets and a receipt.

Jonah led the two of them up the beach to a half-rotted bulk of wood that had obviously been washed up at some point and left in the part of the beach that the tides no longer reached.

"I love driftwood," Jonah proclaimed.

"You do?" Lias asked, puzzled by the statement. "Why is that?"

"The life of driftwood is a great message," Jonah responded. "Driftwood is born at sea, born of something not of the sea. It finds itself tossed in the elements, weathering storms that might sink the strongest of boats. Sun beats down on it, marine life attacks it, and the sea's salt attempts to rot it, yet it perseveres. At some point, the sea gets tired of trying and expels it onto the shore.

In its new home, driftwood provides shelter for animals, and sometimes, people break it into pieces. When set aflame, driftwood burns in shades of blue, green, and lavender, though its fumes are toxic. But even in death, driftwood never gives up. I wish I was as strong as driftwood."

Clearly impressed (but not surprised) by his husband's poeticism, Lias stood there a second, standing atop the battered log. "You don't have to be that strong, silly," he said. "Unlike a piece of driftwood, eternally floating at sea, you're not alone against the elements. You have a wonderful boyfriend!"

"Husband," Jonah corrected, smiling.

"Husband," Lias agreed, leaning in for a kiss as the tattered bright red Jungle Jeep pulled up to collect them.

The rugged vehicle seemed to effortlessly climb into every inch of the island that Lias had always hoped to see. The winding trails up the mountainside were bumpy but beautiful. The jeep intentionally hydroplaned as it slid through the water-covered grassy knolls, while most of the time it kept spitting out dust as it made its way up the steep curves.

"It's everything I always imagined it to be," Lias gloated.

Jonah nodded, his words difficult to find amidst his uneasiness with the lack of traction on the tires of the vehicle they were in.

The winds blew between the newlyweds as their jeep flew across the sand dunes, while at the same time, the sun began to set on their first night. The back of the jeep spun around as they skidded to a stop before a huge circle of people gathered on the beach. In the center of the crowd, a local drum circle wailed in front of an enormous fire. The rainbow-colored flames seemed to spit into the evening air before disappearing.

"Is that a driftwood fire?" Lias asked, his irises painted in the colors of the flames.

"That it is," Jonah confirmed. "I told you they were beautiful."

The flames danced in a frenzy in response, as if celebrating the couple's union with them.

TWELVE

very muscle in Lias' body ached as he pounded the ground with his feet. With each step, his mind tried to justify if the two-hour hike to the mountaintop was worth the stunning view. Though he enjoyed being outdoors, his body was reaching its limits of exhaustion.

Jonah, ever the considerate one, had made sure they took in all the sights of the area that Lias had always dreamed of seeing. Lias was beginning to think that a low-key day was in order, as he desperately needed some time to rest and recover.

"I made reservations at a Brazilian steak house for dinner while you were in the shower this morning," Jonah suggested. "I figured we could stock up on protein and then take it easy tomorrow. I know I could use a break from all this walking."

"As long as that's what you want," Lias replied.

The offer was music to Lias' ears, and relief flooded his body like a tidal wave. *Let the resting be his idea, not mine*, Lias thought to himself, suppressing a smile and a gentle nod of agreement. Lias was usually the more athletic one, but he found himself struggling to keep up with Jonah's seemingly endless supply of energy.

Maybe I'm overdoing it with the carbs for breakfast, Lias mused. The hotel provided a selection of breads and pastries from around the world, and it was too hard to resist. He had to make sure his always-empty stomach was full enough for the day's activities, which had become more frequent lately.

At last, Lias reached the bottom of the mountain. "Let's catch back up to the Jeep, I want to see the waterfalls again before we head back."

He had actually meant it as a ploy for a rest but had hoped Jonah wouldn't realize. Waiting for the jeep tour would be an excuse for him to sit down, and it would drop them off right next to the resort.

"Sounds great!" Jonah exclaimed. "They were beautiful yesterday. It would be great to see them again."

The bumpy ride in the Jungle Jeep started out annoying today, but now, with the jungle shade blocking the sun and the air cooling his face, Lias welcomed the experience. The Jeep moved along a dirt trail, close enough for them to feel the mist of the waterfalls. Lias outstretched his hand to catch some of the cool droplets and splash them on his face.

"You ok?" Jonah asked, clearly having noticed Lias' faintness.

"Yes," Lias murmured. "I think the last of breakfast has worn off."

"I figured we would miss lunch with the hike," Jonah said. "I made early bird dinner reservations."

"Thank God," Lias said with a grateful smile. The thought of food, and soon, brought genuine but short-lived happiness to his mood.

The always-excited tour guide was mumbling something about the waterfalls and the way they were formed over millions of years, but Lias had trouble making it out. It took all his focus to concentrate on his equilibrium and ignore the rocking and swaying of the weightless jeep that he'd enjoyed so much the day before. It was giving him a spell of vertigo.

"Incredible," Jonah said in response to the information shared over the jeep's PA system. He was temporarily occupied with his camera, taking pictures that would surely be memorable later. Normally, Lias preferred Jonah to live in the moment instead of trying to document it. But in this situation, he was glad Jonah hadn't noticed his momentary struggle.

No way, Lias thought, *can I let him know that I got carsick on our honeymoon*. He tried to focus his mind on something else, anything to distract him from the jeep's motions. He thought about all the amazing sites the island had to offer, both seen and yet to be seen.

But this wasn't helping either. With each scenic vision that came to his mind, his memory bounced along in tune with the jeep's rockiness as each sight was visited.

Then Lias tried to focus on Jonah and the life they were beginning together. But just like before, no matter what he remembered about his husband, it all ended with them on a honeymoon ride on a bouncing jeep.

Finally, something more primal kicked in. A mighty rumble formed in Lias' stomach and made him aware that his breakfast was gone and his stomach was still hungry. As he recalled all the food options available for breakfast, the aromas of each hung strongly in the air around him. His focus was now on food, and the dizziness quickly dissipated.

After thinking about all the great food the hotel had to offer for breakfast, Lias began dreaming of all the potential foods he would have for their early bird dinner. The smorgasbord his mind was creating was sure to exceed that of any restaurant known to man.

In his imagination, every item of his favorite food—be it breakfast, lunch, dinner, or dessert—were all prepared to perfection. Not a single element of a single item was less than pristine. A second grumble from Lias' stomach made this one noticeable to Jonah, and the jeep came to a halt.

"Well, I guess it's a good thing dinner is our next stop on the list," Jonah said with a wink.

"Glad someone's paying attention," Lias replied, before Jonah got one last shot of their beloved island.

THIRTEEN

Lias lay motionless, content with his now full stomach. If Jonah held up his end of their deal, now would be a chance for Lias to get some of the rest he had been promised.

"Do you want to join me in the shower?" Jonah asked with a mischievous wink.

"Not a chance," Lias responded, "You had your chance this morning."

"Your loss," Jonah replied with a chuckle before disappearing into the bathroom.

The sound of the water rhythmically cascading against the tempered glass was enough to make the temptation from the sandman, keeper of dreams, impossible to resist. Lias allowed his eyes to drift shut.

When his sore body woke him up sometime later, Lias scanned the room to realize that he was alone. He felt around the bed for his phone.

What time is it? Lias wondered. *Where is Jonah?*

The time on his phone declared it 1 p.m. Half the day had already passed. Jonah had kept his word and allowed Lias to sleep.

"Thank you very much," Jonah's loud voice echoed down the hall as he opened the door to their hotel suite.

"Have a good time with that bellboy?" Lias questioned.

"Well, that was the plan," Jonah replied. "But on the way to find him, I ran into the nicest young woman and her husband down the hall who are also here on their honeymoon."

"So, you're bi now?" Lias jested, raising a questioning eyebrow.

"Don't be silly, honey," Jonah smirked, leaning over to give Lias a kiss. "Who has the energy to juggle two partners?"

Lias swiped at his husband with a tightly gripped pillow. The chuckle leaving Jonah's lips was not the desired response.

"A peace offering then," Jonah chuckled as he turned to retrieve a covered plate of pastries.

Lias quickly snatched a muffin, almost inhaling the wrapper itself.

"Slow down there, Mr.," Jonah instructed. "These are all for you, no need to choke on them."

"I am starving," Lias retorted between munches. "So, what exactly were you thanking Mr. and Mrs. Honeymoon for?"

"Well," Jonah began, "they caught me staring at brochures in the lobby. I was telling them how quickly everything got put together for our wedding and how we didn't even know until just a few days ago that we would be coming here, and how I didn't want us to miss anything the island had to offer." Lias nodded to show he was listening, but he was unwilling to empty his mouth long enough to respond.

"The wife told me they had signed up months ago for scuba diving," Jonah continued. "There were no brochures for it in the lobby, but she gave me all the information about where they were booked. I figured I would go and see if there is any room for two more. I know how much you love marine life and figured you would enjoy the chance to get up close and personal with some of it."

"Would have been a great career choice for me if I could stand smelling like the sea all day," Lias added.

"Best you stick to those nice clean computers then, huh?" Jonah teased.

"Exactly," Lias agreed. "I can do my work from the comfort of my clean home. It's a win-win. Besides, without me keeping those nice clean computers running, you wouldn't be able to do all that ghostwriting you love so much."

"It pays the bills and I love you for it," Jonah said with a wink. "Do you want to come with me to check out the scuba place, or do you need to hibernate longer?"

"I'll come with you," Lias beamed, passing back the empty plate. "My whole body is sore from laying still so long. The movement will do me some good."

* * *

As they strolled along the beach, the afternoon sun warmed Lias' aching muscles. He had been carrying his shoes for some time, and the long walk made his feet sore. Trying to put them back on would have been too painful.

After what seemed like an eternity, the walk gave way to a marina. The boys strolled down the wooden planks, which were covered in sand, following the directions Jonah had acquired along the way.

"Messieurs!" a young voice called out as they passed by what was once the SS Minnow. "Are you looking for an adventure on the deep sea? No one knows these waters better than me!"

"You're awfully young to be captaining such a dangerous mission," Jonah remarked, eyeing the tiny captain's deep bronze skin and cropped, frizzy black hair.

"I'm 18, sir," the confident young captain replied. "I've lived my whole life on this sea. Have you met another captain with 18 years of experience today?"

"No, we haven't," Jonah replied, returning the enthusiastic smile. "But the day is still young. What's your name, skipper?"

"Captain," he corrected. "I'm Riel. No matter how long your day is, you won't find a better ship or a better crew to make your honeymoon more memorable."

Jonah raised an eyebrow in curiosity. "How do you know it's our honeymoon?" he asked.

"It's my job to know these things," Riel answered. "But anyone could see the way you two move together. The affection is so thick in the air it's almost overwhelming, like bad cologne. That level of love screams newlyweds."

"Hopefully when we get out on the sea, the smell will air out," Jonah joked, eliciting a gentle elbow from his husband.

"Hopefully not," Riel admitted with a grin. "Some of us like the smell."

"Thank you for the offer," Jonah said sweetly, "but we have an appointment."

Jonah and Lias said their goodbyes to Riel and continued on their way, Lias' arm looped through Jonah's.

"He's awfully young to be trying to work the tourists," Lias commented once they were out of earshot.

"18 is not that young," Jonah replied.

"That kid is no more 18 than I am 45," Lias countered. "I'd bet he's 16!"

Good thing I like those older men," Jonah said playfully, winking at his husband.

* * *

The receptionist, hidden behind her oversized sunglasses, offered a friendly apology. "I'm sorry, but we're all booked up here. We're the only scuba school on this side of the island, and we tend to book weeks in advance."

Jonah desperately asked, "Is there anything you can do?"

"I can take down your information and give you a call if something opens up," she replied. "But I have to be honest—there are two other couples already ahead of you waiting for the same call."

Lias watched as Jonah's body tensed, his disappointment evident. Ever since his first trip to SeaWorld as a young boy, Lias had been captivated by the idea of the entire world that lay just beneath the surface of the water. His childhood snorkeling had only given him a glimpse of this hidden world, and he desperately wanted to explore it further.

Without saying a word, Jonah grabbed Lias' hand and led him out of the office and back down the marina. Both men were filled with frustration—Jonah for not being able to provide Lias with the gift he had wanted for so long, and Lias for not being able to satisfy his lifelong fascination.

Riel, the overly perceptive young captain, called out, "Divorced already? I wouldn't have invited you onto the sea if I'd known you two were planning to split up the same day."

"Not quite," Jonah answered. "Just bummed out, that's all."

"Nothing on this island should bring you unhappiness," Riel said.

Lias took this as his chance and asked, "You've lived here your whole life, right? Do you know of any other scuba schools? We were hoping to go diving, but the others are all full."

"Of course I do," Riel said, jumping to his feet. "The *Driftwood* doesn't just do fishing trips. She can take you to places to dive that little school could never dare go. You'll see things you'll never see with any other ship."

"You named your boat after rotten wood?" Lias asked, recalling the story Jonah had shared about driftwood just a few days before.

"Driftwood is not rotten wood," Riel corrected, his voice edged with emotion. "Driftwood is born at sea. It's a safe harbor for birds, fish, and other animals. Driftwood braves the sea until it's ready to come home to shore."

"He meant no offense," Jonah interjected. "This is mostly my fault. I recently did a very poor job of explaining to him what driftwood was."

"There is no boat in the marina more experienced than the *Driftwood*," Riel said, now his voice clear and confident. "She always returns safely. I can take you both diving and show you the wonders that lie beneath the sea, places that no other ship can take you."

Lias never felt so excited. He couldn't believe this chance would now be his. "You're a scuba instructor?" he asked tentatively.

"No," Riel answered. "But there are no laws that say I have to be, or that you have to attend a class to dive. All you need is a boat to take you there. These waters do not belong to man, and what happens in them cannot be dictated by government. If you want to dive, meet me here at sunrise and I will take you."

Jonah opened his mouth to say something, but the stern set of Lias' jaw and the piercing look he gave him stopped Jonah in his tracks. "We will be here," Lias said firmly.

"Great," Riel responded. "I'll bring your gear, and you two bring lunch, cash, and an open mind."

FOURTEEN

Jonah paced around the room in a frantic state, unable to focus his mind. He watched in disbelief as Lias moved around the room with careless ease, getting ready as if today were no different from any other. But this day was far from ordinary. The plan Lias devised was one of the most reckless ideas yet.

"I can't believe we're actually doing this," Jonah said in a shaky voice, for what felt like the millionth time in the last twelve hours.

All night with this, Lias thought remembering the dozens of times Jonah's fear caused him to wake Lias with a new set of concerns. Very little actual sleep occurred.

"Baby, we're not just considering this," Lias reminded him. "We made the decision after talking all throughout last night."

Jonah searched his mind for an argument, any angle that he hadn't thought of in the hours of debating the night before, that could possibly stop this train in its tracks. But he knew deep down that nothing he could come up with would change Lias' mind now. Once he had his mind made up to do something, nothing ever did.

Jonah was the practical one, always seeing the dangers in the world and the realities of what could happen. Lias, however, saw the world as a place of endless opportunities. If you didn't do something because it was scary, then you'd be missing out on all the amazing things the world had to offer. Today, he had a chance to see something he'd always dreamed of, and he wasn't going to let a little fearmongering from the overly rational Jonah stop him.

"But," Lias continued, "You don't have to come. That's your choice, and I understand if you don't want to do it. This is something I really want to do."

Lias knew that the words he just spoken weren't entirely true. Yes, Jonah had the freedom to make his own decision, but Lias also knew that there was no way Jonah would ever choose not to take part in this adventure. They had been through enough together for Lias to be certain of that.

"So, what am I supposed to do?" Jonah asked. "You want me to sit on the boat and wait to see if you come back in one piece? To wonder if a shark found you to be a tasty snack or an eel decided to electrocute you, or if you got trapped in a field of coral?"

"Well, I'm sure a shark would eat me before you," Lias joked. "There's already enough salt in the sea. A little sugar would be a delicacy for him."

"That's not funny," Jonah protested.

"It is funny, my love," Lias corrected. "You saw the numbers online just as I did. Less than ten people worldwide were killed by sharks last year. I'm sure I'm not tasty enough for a random shark in a random part of the sea to bother with."

Jonah had done his own research late into the night, checking site after site for conflicting information. Despite the low odds, those were still odds, and Jonah didn't like odds. The chances of his father being the first fatality at his job were low too...

but he knew he couldn't use that defense. It would be an incredibly low blow to use on their honeymoon to get his way.

"I read the articles," Jonah answered, "but I still don't feel comfortable with this."

"You know what else you didn't feel comfortable with?" Lias asked. "Skydiving, but you wrote so many beautiful things after that experience, things that changed your viewpoint on life forever."

"It did," Jonah agreed.

"And you didn't feel comfortable getting into a hot air balloon without any safety equipment. I remember for weeks you wouldn't stop talking about the majestic sunrise we observed over the cloud index, watching the world come to life beneath our feet."

Jonah nodded in agreement.

"You didn't feel comfortable hang gliding either but look how many times you've wanted to do it again since the first time."

"That's all true," Jonah admitted, "But those were all above land, not below."

"Above, below, it makes no difference," Lias corrected. "They were all dangerous situations that you didn't initially want to do but found value in doing them once you pushed past the fear."

Jonah's eyes widened in understanding, but he had no argument left. He knew that Lias was right; after every scary experience, there was always so much beauty in the world to uncover. Today would likely be no different.

"Today you have yet another opportunity to see something so many others will never get to see. You'll be able to write firsthand about things that other authors can only imagine. You'll have an experience some people would give anything to have," Lias said.

"Okay, okay," Jonah relented. "Let's spend our last day of this honeymoon doing something amazing that scares the hell out of me."

As Jonah's pacing slowed, Lias leaped towards him, tumbling them both onto the gigantic bed.

"Why don't we see about calming those nerves a bit before we leave?" Lias suggested with a knowing smile, leaning down for a passionate kiss.

"I'm feeling better already," Jonah replied with a smile of his own.

"Then my work here is done," Lias winked, pulling back slightly.

"Not quite," Jonah corrected, rolling so that he was now pinning Lias beneath him. "I still have a few other nerves that need to be worked."

* * *

The boys hustled across the beach, their faces stinging in the chill of the early morning air as it blew in from the sea.

"Hurry up," Lias urged. "We're going to miss him, you had to spend time downloading those diving tutorials. Where's your sense of adventure?"

"We'll be fine," Jonah countered. "I doubt there's a line of people waiting at sunrise for a kid to take them out for an illegal dive. We need to have some training before we get into the water anyway."

"You'd better be right," Lias huffed, his breaths coming out in short bursts.

"I am," Jonah replied confidently. "No point in being reckless with our recklessness."

Lias shook his head at his husband's absurd remark, too tired from the jog to argue. The backpack of snacks thumped against his back as he sprinted across the lumpy sand toward the marina.

"Good morning," Riel greeted, waving at the approaching men. "I was wondering what was keeping you, but from the look on your faces, I'm not wondering anymore."

Lias shot an annoyed glance at Jonah, who was grinning like a bobcat at the young man's astuteness.

"You know there's plenty of more lucrative jobs in psychology for someone as observant as you," Jonah said, shaking hands with Riel.

"I'm sure you're right," Riel replied, "but none of them would let me spend my days in the place that makes me the happiest: out on the sea with my favorite lady." He patted his boat affectionately.

Lias tuned out the small talk, his gaze drifting out over the vast expanse of water they were about to traverse. *What secrets does it hold?* he wondered. *Treasures that would make me rich beyond my wildest dreams? New creatures? A secret language among its inhabitants?*

Lias let his mind wander, imagining the possibilities with a childlike optimism.

"Sign your life away," Jonah said, thrusting a clipboard with a personal injury and death waiver in front of Lias.

Lias looked up at his husband's comment, seeing a hint of excitement in his eyes. *He's teasing me*, Lias thought. *He's just as excited as I am, but he doesn't want to show it.*

"Permission to come aboard, Captain," Jonah said, handing the signed clipboard back to young Riel.

"Granted," Riel smiled. "Welcome aboard the *Driftwood.*"

FIFTEEN

Lias rolled his eyes as Jonah, for the fifteenth time, went over what each piece of gear was called and how they would use it. A few online videos, and he considered himself an expert. Lias pretended to be attentive and engaged, knowing that this was just who Jonah was. If they were going to be able to enjoy today's activity, he'd have to play along.

"How do you clear your mask," Jonah asked.

"Do I have to wear a mask for this?" Lias teased. "I don't usually put anything over my face unless it's Halloween, and I don't see any ghosts around here."

"Be serious," Jonah directed. "It's important."

"Fine," Lias surrendered. "I take a breath, hold the mask tight at the top, and then I exhale through my nose while tilting my head back."

"Show me," Jonah instructed, tossing Lias a mask.

After a few comical moments of pretending to not know how to wear the mask properly, Lias complied so they could move on to whatever boy scout preparedness was next on his husband's list.

"Show me how to equalize pressure in your ears," Jonah instructed.

Lias tilted his head to the right and patted his left ear with the palm of his left hand over and over, pretending to drain something from his right ear.

"No," Jonah said.

In silence, Lias widened his eyes and pointed sternly to the sky, as if to say, I have an idea. Then he twisted both index fingers into his ears.

"Be serious," Jonah pleaded.

"Fine," Lias huffed, before pinching his nose and making a show of blowing against it, as if his eyes were being pushed out of their sockets by the pressure building inside his skull.

"Remember, as we go down farther, it's necessary to do that often," Jonah reminded.

Lias tried to stay engaged as Jonah fumbled down a checklist for each piece of equipment and how to use each, over and over again. However, it was hard for Lias to concentrate as the marina disappeared and they were surrounded by the vast open sea. It was impossible to focus on clearing the regulator or achieving neutral buoyancy when the great unknown beckoned him from just below his feet.

"Okay, okay, enough of the heavy stuff," Lias finally exclaimed. "I didn't sign up for this class and I want a refund."

"Your safe return to shore will be the refund from this class," Jonah said, raising his voice slightly and pointing back towards the hotel.

"I got it, safety first," Lias agreed. "But if you go over the same stuff one more time, I'm going to jump overboard and let a shark eat me." Jonah's scowl told Lias that his humor was not appreciated now.

"If you boys are done with class, we are here," Riel interjected.

Lias jumped to his feet, eager to get going. Riel helped the two suit up.

"It's only about fifteen feet from the ship to the ocean floor here. It's an ideal spot for you to get used to the feeling of being underwater. If anything doesn't feel right, just swim back up to me. The tank holds enough air for about fifty-five minutes, so keep an eye on the time. I have three more sites to explore depending on how long you spend at the first one," Riel instructed.

"We've come all this way out, and we're only fifteen feet from the bottom?" Lias asked, incredulously.

"Don't let the ocean fool you," Riel replied. "It's not flat. There are valleys and peaks everywhere."

"Got it," Jonah said. "We'll keep an eye out. Thanks."

Jonah hadn't finished speaking before Lias made a splash behind them, signaling that the time for conversation was over. Jonah secured his mask and dove in, his heart pounding with anticipation of what he'd see when he broke the surface of the water.

Adrenaline coursed through Lias' veins as he descended quickly to the ocean floor. Despite his annoyance with Jonah's last-minute lessons, he was thankful that he knew how to properly clear his mask and how to equalize his ears.

I guess I have to thank Jonah for his lesson on buoyancy later, Lias thought. *It's cool to be able to just hover in place and not miss anything. I definitely wouldn't have figured that out on my own. But no need to give him that satisfaction right now. That can be a gift for later.*

Something tugged at Lias' memory as he turned around, and he saw Jonah struggling to master the practical use of those lessons. *Typical*, Lias thought. *Book smarts only get you halfway there.* Action gives you the rest. He gestured for Jonah to join him and help him get control over his buoyancy. The irony of that thought wasn't lost on him. Jonah's intelligence, combined with Lias' action-first attitude, created the perfect balance for each other. They created buoyancy with each other.

Once Jonah was more or less under control, Lias was able to take in the ocean floor. A school of tiny gray and blue striped fish swam past them, unafraid of their presence. The sun's rays shone brightly on the sand, creating a pattern that reminded Lias of broken glass. Patches of small coral and plant life were scattered around.

It's beautiful, Lias thought, but there aren't any secrets to be found in this kiddie pool. He practiced moving around and was about to head back to the boat when Jonah signaled that it was time to go back to the surface.

"How was it, boys?" Riel asked as he reached an arm down to help them both back onto the *Driftwood.*

"It was okay," Lias said, removing his mask. "I was hoping to see a bit more though."

"This stop wasn't about seeing," Riel replied. "It was about experiencing. I can't exactly take you to the middle of the ocean and just drop you off, can I? That would be terribly irresponsible of me."

"Thank you," Jonah answered. "We really appreciate everything you're doing to make this as memorable as possible. This might be our only chance to ever go scuba diving."

"Yes, thank you," Lias added, feeling embarrassed for his earlier comment. "I didn't mean to sound ungrateful."

"The next stop is still about the feeling, but there'll be more to see, I promise," Riel assured them.

*   *   *

After their second dive, Lias needed to refuel. He had already eaten a full sandwich, and he watched his partner scribble away in a notebook that had somehow found its way into the snack-filled backpack.

He never takes enough time for himself, Lias thought. *Always worrying about what his characters are doing on the page. I can almost see it now: his protagonist is seeing, for the first time, the orange and white striations of the crowded school of fish, swimming across the coral-covered ocean floor we just experienced. He should take more time to be in the moment and less time on the pages of his notebook.*

Lias crumpled his wrapper and tossed it, striking his distracted husband in the neck.

"Oops, sorry!" Jonah apologized. "I didn't expect to be so inspired today. I've never been so captivated by the ocean as I am today. If I don't jot down these thoughts, I may lose them."

Meanwhile, Riel looked back, his youthful face complemented by the glimmering sunlight dancing on the ocean's surface.

"Looks like you have about 27 minutes left in your tanks," Riel confessed. "That's not enough time for the two dives I have planned."

"Can you take us to the spot with the most to see in that time?" Lias asked.

"I can," Riel said. "But it's a deeper dive. Are you sure you're up for it? It's about sixty feet down, but it's teeming with life."

"Sold," Lias replied.

Jonah shot his partner an uneasy look, but the determination in Lias' eyes told him there was no dissuading him. He shook his head and kept his words to himself.

Lias was soaking up the afternoon sun when Riel cut the engine and announced they had reached their final destination. Once again, Lias was the first to suit up and prepare to jump overboard.

"Remember," Riel instructed, "this dive will take you deeper. Keep an eye on your air tank and take your time to get back. We're in the depths of the ocean and you may witness a variety of underwater life. Be respectful; this is their home."

Plunging into the depths, Lias was awestruck by the beauty of his surroundings. He didn't want to miss a moment, so he furiously flapped his fins to reach the ocean floor. He was overtaken by a school of fish as if he were invisible. He spotted turtles, jellyfish, and countless vibrant creatures in the depths.

This is where it all happens, he thought. *This is where the secrets lie. Not even movies can express the magnificence of the plant life here—it's simply mesmerizing.*

Something else caught Lias' eye. It seemed to be an underground tunnel. Curiosity drove him to take a closer look, and he was suddenly reminded of Ariel's voice. What wonders lie hidden behind the walls of this cavern?

Entering the tunnel, Lias completely forgot about the outside world. He was captivated by the lush vegetation and small fish swimming in and out. He ran his gloved hands along the sea garden, imagining how each one felt—soft, squishy, fuzzy. The coral seemed to beg to be touched and Lias had to oblige. He was entranced by the beauty of the unknown.

Ouch, he recoiled as the sharp coral caught his palm, slicing through his wet suit. He tightened his grip as the salt stung his skin. He was angry with himself for not being more careful. What will Jonah think about this, he fretted; this wasn't covered in the training. *Jonah. I completely forgot about Jonah! Better go see how he's enjoying his last few minutes down here.*

Lias took a final mental image of the tunnel before heading out to meet up with Jonah. As he swam closer, he noticed a hammerhead shark circling his friend. Jonah remained still, watching the curious creature without movement.

At the same time, the shark noticed Lias' emergence. It lowered its nose like a bloodhound catching a scent. Lias clenched his fists, as he realized what was about to happen. He remembered the only thing he remembered learning about sharks. *If one attacks, stand your ground and punch it in the nose as hard as you can.*

The shark seemed to grow angry as it circled Jonah a final time before its dorsal fin sliced through the water like a sharp blade directed at Lias. Its intimidating presence caused a ripple of fear throughout the depths of the ocean as it moved.

Its menacing black eyes watched Lias, its jaw unhinging and its gills puffing in anger. Its tail thrashed the water, creating a wake of churning foam as it moved closer and stirring up a swirling cloud of sand that momentarily obscured Jonah from sight. Its eyes burned with rage, and its tail thrashed back and forth as it approached, ready to attack.

Lias knew he had to act quickly, and his instinct kicked in. He surged through the water towards his husband intercepting the shark's path. His powerful legs kicked out with each stroke, drawing the shark's attention. He felt the adrenaline course through his veins as the shark neared. He clenched his fist, readying himself for the fight, and with all the force he could muster, he punched the shark straight in the nose.

The shark paused, its beady eyes studying Lias with a sudden intensity, as he threw a second punch. Realizing that Lias was not an easy meal, it swiftly glided away, its powerful tail propelling it through the murky depths at an astonishing speed. Lias hovered there motionless, watching its silhouette become ever more distant until it vanished from sight.

Lias, his heart still racing with adrenaline, scanned the ocean for Jonah, but all he could see was a vast expanse of blue. He hastily scanned the waters for any sign of his beloved husband, but there was nothing. Panic began to set in as he desperately searched for any sign of life.

Suddenly, Lias caught a glimpse of something floating atop the surface of the water. He swam closer and his heart sank as the shape of Jonah came into focus. Realization struck as Lias swam toward his motionless husband. *In the frantic circling of the shark, Jonah must have been struck by the shark's tail and knocked unconscious.*

Jonah was lifeless, and his body floated flat on the surface, his arms and legs dangling beneath him like a puppet on strings, an enormous shadow cast upon him by the regal-looking *Driftwood*.

SIXTEEN

Lias paced the same strip of hospital waiting room floor for the thousandth time, his frustration building with each stride. Hours had passed since they had taken Jonah back and no one would tell him anything. In the rush to put the wedding together, everything had been quickly arranged at the last minute; there was no record yet of the legitimacy of their marriage.

My own haste got us into this situation, Lias thought, frantically. *We never should have come here. This was my dream vacation, not his. This is all my fault. We didn't even think to bring a copy of our wedding certificates to prove that we're soulmates.*

Lias knew, even as he thought the words, that they weren't true. Even if they somehow were true, Jonah would never see it that way. Right now, he was just angry that they were married. *Married*, and still, no one would acknowledge them as anything more than strangers. As if they hadn't spent every moment together for the last decade.

Irritation grew as Lias glared at the frumpy woman behind the giant nurse's counter who had told him, for the 50th time, that she could not give out any information about Jonah. *If she only knew how easily*— His thoughts were interrupted by some movement at the desk. A new nurse had arrived, clipboard in hand, obviously for shift change. *I'll wait for them to finish and try again once the ogre nurse leaves for the day to go home to her cats.*

Lias focused his attention on the clock on the wall; it had been nearly six hours since he'd seen Jonah. Six hours of torturous waiting. His cellphone had died shortly after arriving; all the attempted calls at sea had drained the battery. Lias was mid-call with his Papa, sharing what was going on, when the battery finally ran out. No one in the waiting room was willing to give up a charger, and Lias was not willing to leave the hospital to retrieve one from their hotel room.

Once he was certain the witch nurse was gone, Lias tried again to get an update on Jonah.

"Ma'am, could you give me an update on Jonah Greene?" Lias asked. "He's my husband."

"Do you have any paperwork, or an ID that can show me that?" the obviously kinder nurse questioned.

"No, we just got married, this is our honeymoon. I didn't imagine needing to prove to anyone that we are a couple," Lias replied, exasperated.

"Then I'm sorry, there is nothing I can do," the obviously sympathetic nurse admitted.

"Actually," a commanding voice interrupted from behind Lias, "you can get me whomever the doctor is in charge of Mr. Greene's care, and you can do so immediately. My office has already called ahead and spoken to your administrator. I am his attorney, and he needs to be prepared to immediately return to Atlanta for further care."

As the man stepped forward and handed some paperwork to the new nurse, she grabbed it, glanced at it quickly, and disappeared just as fast through a set of double doors.

"Dad," Lias said as he fell into his father's arms. "I thought Papa would come. I called him hours ago."

"I had to come anyway," Samuel admitted.

"I don't understand," Lias confirmed.

"I had to come anyway for Jonah. I will explain on the way home. Take my rental, grab your things from the hotel, and meet me back here in an hour. By then the three of us will be headed home," Samuel commanded.

"Dad," Lias whimpered. "I don't even know if he's..."

"Oh honey," Samuel interrupted, not letting Lias even finish his thought. "He's alive, but in a coma. His charts have already been reviewed by his soon-to-be attending and she has cleared him to make the trip home." Samuel's voice left no room for questioning; he was certain. "One hour, son," Samuel reminded, extending out the keys to his rental car. Lias did not question his father further. He grabbed the keys and darted out the door. His father taking charge of the situation brought hope to Lias; *Dad would make sure everything would be okay.*

* * *

Lias rushed through, packing and checking out of the hotel. When he drove back up to the hospital, he saw his father, Samuel, already outside on the phone. His posture was tense and determined—a side of Samuel that Lias had never seen before. He was reminded how, at work, his dad was a relentless force, always fighting for justice for his clients. For the first time, Lias was thankful that his father was so dedicated to his job. Though he still had no idea why Samuel had come.

Samuel made a familiar gesture—a circular motion with his fingers—indicating that he would be driving and Lias should exchange places with him. Without hesitation, Lias hopped out of the car and into the passenger seat.

"Good," Samuel said, pocketing his phone before getting into the driver's seat.

"Dad, what's going on?" Lias asked anxiously.

"I love you, son. I'm here for you, of course, but I'm also here as Jonah's legal counsel. I'm here to make sure that his medical wishes are followed," Samuel explained.

"What wishes? And since when does Jonah have legal counsel?" Lias queried.

"Shortly after his mother began to decline, Jonah asked me to help him draft his medical directives, in case he ever found himself in the same situation. Being the last of his family, I told him it was wise and important to do so. I helped him prepare all the documents and he's kept me on retainer for the past eight years for the sum of one dollar per month, prepaid in advance," Samuel replied.

Why didn't you tell me about this before?" Lias questioned.

"Attorney-client privilege. Before you two were married, his medical directives weren't something I was at liberty to share with you. I just assumed that there was plenty of time for him to tell you himself," Samuel said.

Lias was overwhelmed by this new information. His body had been put through so much in the last few hours and now this was threatening to break him.

"What are his directives?" Lias finally managed to ask, realizing he had overlooked the most important questions. *What did Jonah want?* Lias thought, unable to recall a single conversation they had had around the subject.

"Well," Samuel began, "he appointed me as his power of attorney to make sure that if something were to happen to him, his mother would still be taken care of for as long as necessary." Lias nodded attentively.

"He also had me set up a medical proxy to make any necessary medical decisions for him in the unlikely event that he is unable to. We've been in touch all day, and she felt it best to get him back to Atlanta, where she would have complete control over his care."

"She?" Lias asked, boggled.

"Sorry, yes," Samuel confirmed. "I should have clarified. Jonah asked that Eternity be in charge of his care if he were unable to make choices for himself. He felt that it was impossible for anyone without a medical degree to have enough knowledge to accurately make medical decisions. He was also very clear that he did not intend to burden you in particular with those decisions."

Lias felt his heart tighten at hearing those words. "He didn't trust me to make his decisions," Lias whispered.

"It has nothing to do with trust," his father countered. "Jonah was absolutely right, no one outside of a medical professional would have enough inside information to analyze risks and make an informed medical decision in the worst of scenarios. For what it's worth, after talking to Jonah, your father and I both elected Eternity to be our medical proxy as well. And you know I trust your father with my life."

That is true, Lias thought.

"It just makes me feel useless though. You know?" Lias shared.

"You are far from useless, baby," Samuel said with confidence. "You have the most important role of us all. There is no one else in the world with a higher chance of pulling Jonah out of this than you. Stay focused on that. Your job is to let him know that you are there, that you are present."

SEVENTEEN

*hy **Jonah***? Lias thought as he stood outside Jonah's room, the first time he had been able to be near him since medical personnel had taken him away. *There was no one more special than him alive in this world.* The comfort of his father's presence allowed Lias to rest briefly on the flight home. They had come straight from the airport.

"What does 'DNR' mean?" Lias asked, seeing the paper brightly displayed outside Jonah's door.

"It means 'Do Not Resuscitate'," Samuel replied. "One of Jonah's directives was that if his heart stopped beating or he stopped breathing, he did not want to be brought back to life 'artificially.'"

"Why wouldn't he want to live no matter what?" Lias asked, his anger rising inexplicably.

"Do you remember the ice storm a few years ago when Vivian was electrocuted while trying to save that boy?" Samuel said.

"Of course I do," Lias answered, not understanding the connection between the two events.

"Well, when she was shocked her heart stopped. Paramedics were able to revive her with CPR," Samuel explained.

"Thankfully," Lias said.

"Yes, thankfully," Samuel agreed. "But from that day on, Jonah felt that she started to feel different. Her thoughts were hazy, she became increasingly confused, and then she would have occasional periods where she would completely lose herself."

Lias stared at his father, desperately trying to take in every word and comprehend what it had to do with Jonah now.

Samuel's voice softened as he continued, "Jonah felt that when she 'died,' the part of her that held everything together didn't come back when her body started working again. He believed that her brief time being dead was the beginning of her decline. He didn't want that for himself, so he took measures to ensure he wouldn't follow the same path as his mother."

"I knew he was scared of walking in her footsteps, but I didn't realize it was like this," Lias admitted. "But I can't just let him die and do nothing. How can I fight that?"

"Well, as Jonah's attorney, you cannot fight that. His instructions are legally binding. No one can force him to do something he clearly didn't want. As your father, you shouldn't want to fight it either. Even though you are shocked by this, this is how Jonah chose to live his life. As his partner, you must allow him, even now, to make his own choices. Even if you don't agree with them or if they hurt you."

"I can't, I won't do anything," Lias challenged.

Samuel pulled his son close, wrapping both arms around his son's as he spoke. "Do you remember when we had to move to Nebraska when you were little?"

"Yes," Lias answered.

"That was not my choice, and it was the last place I ever wanted to be with you kids. Your father told me he had to go away, and I might not ever see him again. I loved him, and I didn't want him to go, but I trusted him. I knew that if he felt this was what he had to do, then it had to be the right thing for him. It broke my heart to honor his request, but I had to." Samuel now held his son with one hand on each shoulder, looking deeply into his eyes.

"But I don't want him to go," Lias wept.

"He hasn't gone anywhere, son," Samuel corrected. "He is right through those doors, waiting for you. Just remember that even though he can't make decisions in real-time, they have already been made. For the choices that he couldn't make in advance, he couldn't have picked a better doctor to make them for him. Your sister loves him just as much as you do, and she has one of the brightest medical minds in the world today. If there is anything that can be done for him, she will do it."

"I know she does, I know she will," Lias said, wiping the tears from his face.

After a moment, the two crossed the threshold and pulled up two chairs next to Jonah's bed. Lias kissed him softly on the forehead, then his lips.

"I love you, and I'm here," Lias whispered quietly as he caressed Jonah's pale face.

Samuel sat watching this interaction. He knew it should be a private, tender moment, but he also knew that this was not a time for his son to be left alone.

The two sat in silence for a while, with Lias holding Jonah's hand until Lias spoke. "Why are there no machines?"

"What do you mean?" Samuel asked, pointing to the monitor next to Jonah, which was displaying his heart rate from a cord attached to his index finger.

"How is he going to eat or drink? Shouldn't there be a machine giving him nutrients?" Lias questioned, his voice rising in confusion.

"Another one of his medical directives," Samuel replied, trying to keep his voice even. "Jonah did not wish to be kept alive through artificial means, including a respirator or a feeding tube."

"*What?*" Lias challenged, standing up. His voice was flustered and angry. "How long can he survive like this without any nutrients going into his body?"

"That depends," Eternity's voice was firm as she walked into the room, followed by a nurse wheeling in an IV bag. Samuel opened his mouth to object, but Eternity spoke first.

"It is just saline to keep him hydrated," She offered. "Nothing in his wishes is being violated. No machine, just gravity."

Samuel eyed the rolling cart that held the saline bags. They were old and antique, not like the automated IV drips you'd expect to see in a hospital now.

"That is a very thin line to walk, Eternity," Samuel reprimanded.

"Dr. Anderson," she corrected, directing her focus back to her father. "As Jonah's doctor and as his medical proxy, this is in his best interest and is a decision within my rights to make."

Samuel instinctively curled his lip back, warning, "Make sure you stay on the right side of that line, Dr. Anderson."

Eternity ignored his comment and turned to hug her brother as the nurse set up the drip for Jonah.

"I am so sorry," she whispered in his ear. "I will do everything that I can."

Lias heard the promise that she could not say aloud in the presence of her father or Jonah's lawyer. She would be as creative as possible in giving Jonah the care he needed, but within the legal boundaries that bound her actions.

"How long can he be like this without machine support?" Lias asked again.

"Not long," Eternity replied. "But now that he's receiving some liquid back into his system, it could be longer."

"How long?" Lias pressed, not content to accept the generic answer. "Don't talk to me as if I'm any other concerned spouse. Talk to me like I'm your brother."

"It can vary a lot," Eternity began, her voice soft. "It usually ranges from eight days to a few weeks, potentially longer, but I don't want to give you false hope."

EIGHTEEN

The incessant jackhammering outside his thin-walled apartment had Lias groaning in frustration as he tugged at his fourth pair of jeans, throwing them into the growing pile in the corner. He grabbed a fifth pair in desperation.

"Well, what did you expect?" Tavia asked, tossing the remnants of food wrappers and pizza boxes into the trash bag she held. "Your metabolism changes as you get older, brother. All you've done for a week is eat, sit, and sleep. Where do you think all that junk food is going?"

"Well—" Lias sighed, giving up and grabbing a pair of sweatpants.

"Well, nothing," Tavia interjected. "No one is saying it's not normal. I'm just pointing out that it's not surprising you can't shovel food into your body like a pie-eating contest every day without any exercise and expect it to magically disappear."

Pie, Lias mulled over the word that usually brought joy to him, but now held static, grabbing a shirt and sliding into a pair of sandals.

"Do you think we have time to grab a slice on the way?" Lias asked trying to seem like himself for his sister. *No reason for her to know that I have no joy at all right now*, Lias thought.

"It's 9 a.m., piggy," Tavia rolled her eyes wondering how her brother could think of food with everything else going on around him. "And we need to be at the home to have Vivian ready by 9:30. You'll have to wait for your breakfast pie."

Lias swiped two pieces of the day-old cold pizza from the box before Tavia tossed it into her now full trash bag. While no food sounded good, Lias found recently that the constant chewing motion did help bring calm to his emotions.

"P.S. Clean up this mess of an apartment," she ordered. "It does no one any good for you to live like this."

Lias shifted uneasily. "Do you think it's a good idea to expose Vivian to this? She's already gone through so much. She probably won't even know who he is."

"We've gone over this," Tavia replied. "Jonah is in bad shape. As his mother, she deserves a chance to see him before..."

Her voice trailed off as her gaze focused forward on the wall ahead.

*　*　*

The sounds of an overcrowded and understaffed hospital filled the air outside of Jonah's room as Lias escorted Vivian in.

"I'll go get us something to drink," Tavia declared, to which Vivian replied with a smile, "Tea for me, honey."

Today had been a good day for Vivian; she remembered Lias' name, though he felt as if she didn't quite know who he was to her. Gently, Vivian asked, "Why are you so sad, sweetie?" As if she were unaware of her sleeping son just a few feet away.

"A close friend of mine is very ill, and I don't think he'll make it," Lias answered, his gaze shifting to Vivian's son.

Vivian followed his eyes for a moment before focusing back on him. "More than a friend, I'd say," she commented, taking note of the way he looked at Jonah.

"A close friend," Lias smiled. He never pushed her, as it was easier to just let the conversation flow and see where it took them. It was almost like interacting with an innocent child.

"You love him," Vivian corrected. "I would bet my bottom dollar on that fact. What's his name?"

"His name is Jonah," Lias replied, a tinge of guilt washing over him as he spoke his name aloud. Already, it was beginning to feel like speaking his name was forbidden.

Vivian kissed Lias' cheek as he sat in the corner of the room, then walked over to the hospital bed. Lias fidgeted in his uncomfortable chair, wishing someone was with him. Vivian stood over Jonah for what seemed like an eternity in silence, until an announcement overhead caused a flurry of activity outside. Medical personnel rushed past the door and down the hall toward another patient, dragging supplies with them as they flew past Jonah's room.

Lias stared, wondering what happened. *What code would be called...how long before they rushed into Jonah's room in the same manner?* Then he remembered the DNR. *No one would be rushing to resuscitate him when his body stops.* Lias corrected his own mind, *if his body stops.*

Some movement in the room caught his attention, bringing his focus back to Jonah. Vivian leaned over, whispering into his ear before kissing his forehead. Nothing was wrong with a mother kissing her son at a time like this, but just moments ago she hadn't known him. This shook Lias.

"Is everything all right, Vivian?" he asked.

His words were a shock to her. The confusion on her face, as she turned to face him, made his heart race. Vivian took a few short, quiet steps toward Lias and took his hand into hers.

"No, my sweet boy, everything is not all right," Vivian answered.

"What is wrong?" Lias probed.

"I really hate to be the one to tell you this. I am really shocked that none of the doctors told you this., but the person you love is not in that body over there."

Lias' eyebrows narrowed above his nose. He was used to her rambling, but this was something he couldn't brush off and move on from. Impossible.

"What do you mean?" he asked.

"Oh, honey," Vivian stared deeply into his eyes. "The person you love is not in that body over there. No one is in there. That is just an empty shell."

NINETEEN

The words rang repeatedly in his head. *What is she talking about?* Lias wondered. *Is it just another one of her moments where she isn't fully there?* He wanted to move past it like he did with any other thing she said that was out of place.

But Lias couldn't let this go. The question lingered in his subconscious. The words he was afraid to think, afraid to ask, and afraid to know for the past week. *Was Jonah still in there?*

His mother-in-law spoke the words he was the most afraid to hear. The words that some part of him knew to be true the moment she said them. She knew what a secret part of him already knew. That was the reason he stopped staying the night in this room a few days ago. *Jonah wasn't in there.*

"Who's thirsty?" Tavia barged in, arms crossed elbow to elbow with drinks and snacks tucked into every possible nook.

"I am," Lias announced, his cheeks reddening as he wiped back a tear.

"Big shocker, little oinker," Tavia teased, tossing a fruit pie across the room at Lias, the closest thing she could find to the breakfast pie he had missed out on.

"Thanks," Lias said, nearly biting through the wrapper as he inhaled the treat.

The morning drifted by, and soon the afternoon started to peek its ugly head.

"We should get Vivian back," Tavia said. "They'll be serving lunch soon."

"Monday's chicken-fried steak and potatoes," Vivian added, grinning.

"Actually," Lias began, "could you take her back alone? I'm not ready to leave yet. I'll catch a ride-share home in a bit." He felt guilty for sitting there all day, agreeing with Vivian that Jonah wasn't actually there. He needed some time alone to process that in private.

"You sure?" Tavia asked, her eyes filled with questions.

"I'm a big boy," Lias reminded her. "I can sit by my husband's bedside without a babysitter."

"Roger that," Tavia said, taking Vivian's hand and leading her out of the room.

As soon as his sister ushered Vivian out of the room and was out of earshot Lias whispered as he held Jonah's hand, "I am sorry I ever thought that I wasn't ready to have the full married life with you. Wake up now and we'll buy a house together tomorrow. Wake up now and I promise I will always mow the grass. Wake up now and ill change the diapers. Please wake up. Please."

Tears rolled down Lias' cheek as the shameful memory of him not feeling ready for a life full of everything with Jonah lingered in his brain. Now, at this moment, anything, everything was on the table if Jonah would just wake up.

As his tears dried Lias sat back down in his chair, scooting it near the foot of Jonah's bed. He finished off the remaining snacks from earlier and heard the swooshing of the busy highway outside. Its rhythmic, hypnotic sound was soothing, and he found himself drifting in and out of consciousness.

* * *

The harsh, salty air filled Lias' senses as he took a bite of his sandwich. The waves rocked the boat, swaying it from side to side. He knew this boat, but he couldn't recall how he had gotten here or why he was now alone. *How did I get here?* he thought. *How do I get back to shore?* He had no idea how to operate a boat or navigate the sea, or in which direction the shore even was.

Lias should have been terrified, yet all he could feel was confusion over why he was there. As he searched the horizon for any sign of life or direction, a loud splash next to the boat startled him. He quickly rose to his feet, ready to defend himself against whatever it was that had made the noise.

A familiar figure wearing a wet suit climbed onto the boat, facing Lias. As the diver removed his gear, Lias lunged forward, ready to take action.

"Jonah! Jonah!" he shouted, embracing his husband tightly.

"Easy there, baby," Jonah soothed, trying to regain his balance. "What's all this emotion about?"

"You've been gone," Lias responded. "I've missed you."

"That's nonsense," Jonah said. "I haven't been gone. I've been right here the whole time."

"You were—you are—" Lias struggled to find the words to explain to Jonah everything that had happened.

"You're getting worked up for nothing," Jonah said. "I was only gone for a few minutes on a dive. It's absolutely stunning down there. I can see why it's always called to you. I could stay here forever—there are so many wondrous things in our world I never knew existed. So many secrets to uncover." As Jonah described the sea, Lias suddenly realized that the words weren't Jonah's—they were his. He was dreaming.

"You're not real," he admitted. "This isn't real."

He looked down, the planks of the boat creaking beneath his feet, slowly dissolving into nothing. He was now standing on a ghostly ship, a translucent vessel that was once known as the *Driftwood*. Its masts and sails were still intact, their billowing fabric caught in the breeze, though he could see right through them. The wood of the hull seemed to be fading away as if it were being carried away by the gentle current. Returning his gaze to Jonah, Lias saw him fading away as well.

"Don't be silly, my love," Jonah said, his voice growing softer. "I will always be right here with you."

Toxic flames of blue, green, and lavender licked the air, consuming the boat and the fading figure of Jonah. Lias felt the heat of the flames as he drew a deep breath and opened his eyes to find himself waking in a world of murky uncertainty.

* * *

A long, annoying beep from Jonah's heart monitor brought Lias back from his dream to the present. His thoughts were still foggy as he looked at the monitor. Tears welled up in his eyes as he saw the straight line and screeching beep indicating Jonah's heart had stopped.

Lias ran to his husband's side, ready to begin CPR that he had learned in Boy Scouts. However, a tight grip on his arm pulled him back.

"You can't," Eternity ordered. "He doesn't want this."

"You can't," Eternity ordered again. Lias, in a fit of panic, tried to pull away from his sister, grasping with flailing arms, but two male nurses now stood between him and Jonah, holding him still.

"I can't do nothing," Lias screeched.

"I am so sorry, Lias," Eternity said in a soothing voice. "It is not up to us anymore. Take him out," she instructed the nurses. "You shouldn't watch."

"I am not leaving him!" Lias yelled, but he threw his hands up to show he wouldn't fight them.

Eternity nodded for the nurses to leave, knowing they wouldn't be able to stop Lias if he truly wanted to fight. As they pulled the door shut, Eternity disconnected the wire from Jonah's index finger. The beeping stopped, and the ringing in Lias' ear paused.

Eternity hugged her brother tightly as he sobbed. She then stepped away, putting her finger to Jonah's neck before glancing up at the wall. Out of instinct, she spoke aloud as she wrote: "Time of death: 12:21 p.m."

TWENTY

An obnoxious pounding from outside his apartment startled Lias awake. The construction crew had been working out there for months, but he still couldn't manage to sleep through it. Without even looking at the clock, he knew it was 8 a.m.; they started right on time every day. He tried to muffle the sound by pressing his pillow tightly over his face. The vibrations added a ringing to the constant tone Lias heard nonstop the last two days since Jonah passed.

"Open up!" Tavia's voice called out, followed by three loud knocks at his door.

Lias groaned.

"Come on, we're going to be late," Tavia insisted.

"No, go away. I'm not going," Lias replied.

Silence answered him. *Was it really that easy?* He wondered. *Did she just accept his wish and go away?*

"Little brother," Tavia started speaking again, and he realized his false hope. Of all his siblings, she would not give up so easily. "Open this door so we can get going."

"No. Go away, I'm not going," Lias insisted.

"Look, I understand today sucks. It sucks for me too, but one way or the other, I'm getting in right now. Either you open this door now, or you replace this door after I split it in half and walk in. Your choice," Tavia challenged.

"You wouldn't," Lias grumbled into his pillow unsure if she could even hear him.

Again, silence. But this time, the silence was a threat. *She's calculating something*, he thought. *How much force she'd need to break the door from its hinges, most likely.*

He knew that she would get in. Lias had seen the tornado that lived inside his impulsive sister. Not even a tank could stop her from getting into his apartment once she set her mind on it.

"Fine," Lias conceded after too many seconds of quiet told him that he was out of time to get this over with the easy way.

"I thought you'd see it my way," Tavia gloated from the other side of the door.

As he opened the door, Tavia was bent over, tucking something back into her sock. Lias wondered what kind of weapon she had hidden away, that she was about to use on his poor door.

"I'm not going. I have nothing that fits. I'm not showing up wearing these sweatpants," Lias said.

"Well, it's a good thing that Dad knew you'd say that," Tavia answered as she retrieved a garment bag hanging on the side rail of his entryway. "He sent you an outfit."

"Of course, he did," Lias protested, refusing to accept the outfit that Samuel had sent.

Lias waved off Tavia as she tried to pass it to him a second time.

"We both know you're going to leave here wearing this. Whether it's polished and beautiful as Dad bought it for you, or if it's in rags after I kick your little butt all over this apartment, is completely up to you," Tavia snarked. "I really have no preference one way or the other."

"Did you at least bring me food?" Lias conceded. Even at his best, he knew he couldn't take on this sister. And he was now far from his best.

"I thought you might require a bribe," Tavia walked outside to retrieve a box of doughnuts she'd left by his door as she prepared to let herself in.

The two stared in silence, sitting across from each other in his kitchen, as Lias scarfed down the third doughnut.

"I don't want to go," Lias spoke softly. This time, his eyes lowered as he spoke the shameful words to his sister. "I already lost him. Why would I want to stand there and be reminded of that?"

"Today is not about losing him," Tavia corrected. "Today is about remembering him. Today is about showing Jonah, friends, and family the level that he touched your life. He deserves that, no matter how much it may hurt you to give it."

Tavia wasn't the soft Anderson. She wasn't a big hugger or a coddler. She was the dry, factual one. It usually bothered him, but the dry truth was what he needed to hear today. His family must have realized that as well, since they elected her to make sure he made it.

"I don't know what to say. I can't—" Lias stuttered.

"It's fine if you don't say a word," Tavia corrected. "It's not about what you say. Your being there says volumes. The words you say, or don't say, today are irrelevant. All that matters is that you're there. You honor him in your own way."

* * *

As Tavia sped away from Lias' apartment complex, he asked her, "What's going on today, exactly?"

"Papa kept it simple," she replied, quickly wiping a tear from her eye. "He figured a closed casket graveside service would be the easiest for everyone. He only wanted our family and Vivian to be there, but—"

Before she could finish her sentence, Lias saw the answer. A row of cars, sharply dressed occupants standing aside them, lined the side of the road. Jonah's friends, family friends, schoolmates, and strangers filled the cemetery. Tavia reached across the car and placed her hand on Lias' shoulder. "Remember, today is about Jonah. Be strong for him. You can do this."

Lias started to tremble, but he nodded.

As they crept past the cars, Lias noticed the onlookers standing far back. His father, brother, and sister each held him in turn, and Lias used the opportunity to wipe his eyes on his brother's shoulder.

Vivian sat at the graveside, quietly staring at the closed casket. Lias told his family he wanted to have a private moment with her, and they lingered back as he approached.

"It's my friend from the hospital," Vivian said, smiling an earnest smile as she rose to hug him. "Hi, honey."

"Hi, Vivian," Lias replied, trying to smile back.

"I know it's so sad about your close friend," she said, hugging him.

"How did you know?" he asked, looking at the casket she couldn't see inside of.

Vivian replied softly, "A blind man doesn't have to see to know the world around him exists."

Lias' eyes widened at the analogy, and he whispered, "I guess not."

"Besides, I may be getting older," Vivian said, "but it's only been a few days since I saw you at the hospital, and today here you are all dressed up talking alone to me while your family is all grouped behind us. I don't have to build rockets to put those clues together."

Lias chuckled. Vivian always knew exactly what to say.

"There's no need to be sad today," she said, caressing the side of his face. "Right there," she pointed at the casket, "is just a box. Your friend isn't there."

"Why do you say that?" Lias asked, taking a deep breath and wiping away a tear.

"Your friend is waiting for you on the *Driftwood*," Vivian answered. "There's no rush for you to get to him, though. His patience is eternal. When it's time for you to meet him, he'll be there."

Lias' heart tightened, his mind racing. *How could she know about the Driftwood?* He hadn't even told his family the name of the boat—they hadn't even told Vivian they were going near the sea.

"How do you know about the *Driftwood*?" he asked.

"I was there, I saw it, honey," she said matter-of-factly. "Your—handsome, by the way—friend told me that he was happy and that there was so much for him to write about now. He told me to tell you not to be sad—it's not good for you now. You have some very important tasks ahead of you."

Lias didn't usually put stock into the ramblings of Vivian's stories, but today she knew something she couldn't possibly know. With a silent breath, he asked, "Did he say anything else?"

But before she could answer, Tavia began to sing loudly and reverently as the family closed the gap to Jonah's graveside. All the emotions she usually struggled to show the world, her softer side, vibrated as the words left her lips. Her voice carried, and Lias could tell by the bowed heads in the distance that the onlookers could hear her crystal clear. As she stepped slowly, she sang the words to "The Prayer" by Celine Dion and Andrea Bocelli.

TWENTY-ONE

Every **bone** in his body ached as Lias struggled to keep up with his sister's boundless energy. The weeks following Jonah's funeral had taken a toll on his slender frame. All he could manage to do was eat and sleep.

"Come on, you slowpoke," Tavia called over her shoulder, watching her brother struggle to make forward progress.

"Go on ahead, I'll catch up," Lias replied, his breath coming in ragged gasps.

"No way," Tavia replied adamantly. "You asked me to help you get back in shape, remember?"

"Yes," he wheezed, mumbling under his breath, "something I'm regretting more and more with every step." He added, "But I can't go back to school like this."

"Then pick up those knees and get moving, Mister!" Tavia commanded.

He wanted to obey her. He wanted to move. She was the only one who could help him regain his strength. But no matter how badly he wanted to keep going, his body refused.

As Lias' pace slowed to a snail's crawl, and he finally stopped to rest on a bus stop bench, Tavia glanced back in frustration, her words too faint for Lias to make out.

He was leaning forward as far as he could without falling over, desperately trying to slow his breathing. His abdomen was aching and cramping in pain.

"You look like you could use a minute in the shade with a tall glass of tea," a kind voice called to him.

Glancing to the side, Lias saw an older woman with round, thick glasses perched atop her head, wearing a white bonnet trimmed with blue lace, who had taken a seat beside him on the bench. He forced himself to sit up straight as he tried to respond.

"It seems like all I've done for the last month or so is eat, drink, and sleep," Lias said, jiggling the little beer belly he had developed in the last few weeks.

"Oh, honey, don't you fret none," the woman replied reassuringly. "I put on the pounds right after my husband died, too. We all do. You'll bounce back." Her words were spoken with absolute certainty.

"How did you know?" Lias asked, now noticing how thin she was.

"Every generation thinks they are going through each experience as the first person to ever come across it," she said, speaking more to herself than to him. "The purple bags under your eyes from lack of sleep, barely disguising the tear-stained red eyes. The way you keep spinning the ring on your finger, even now. I'd wager a tragedy soon after you got married. That ring hasn't been there for very long."

"That's very observant of you, ma'am," Lias replied, relieved by the lack of expectations in their conversation. Everyone around him recently had been so concerned with how he was feeling, he hadn't had the chance to just be.

"Celia will do just fine, thank you," she corrected him, smiling. "I've got plenty of time left in life to be a ma'am."

"Celia," Lias agreed, returning the smile.

"When my William passed, I was in the same situation," Celia said, passing Lias a wrapped candy without asking. "Barely newlyweds when we parted. All I wanted to do was eat, cry, and sleep."

Lias, overwhelmed by the kind gesture, complimented her. "How did you get through it and get back into the very alluring shape you are now so quickly?"

Celia winked, her eyes twinkling. "Well, bless your heart. It was not without a great effort, I tell you. My advice, if you want it," she paused, "is that you must finish breaking first."

"Consider that done," Lias said, pretending to check it off an imaginary list.

"Not quite as easy as that, my dear," Celia said, her voice full of compassion. "When something awful happens in life, like the tragedy you find yourself in now, friends and family immediately rush to your side, hug you, love you. But that's not enough."

Lias looked up at her, confused. "That's not enough?"

"Not a bad thing at all," Celia corrected him, though it was not the only thing he needed. "Imagine you are a beautiful window, clear and letting nothing but beautiful light pass through you every day." Lias nodded as he savored the flavor of the candy in his mouth, content to listen.

"But one day," Celia continued, "something comes crashing into you and you crack all over. That's what life does to us, you know. You're still a window, but now the light reflects off the cracks and is not so beautiful.

"Our family and friends come to try to help, to hug us and tell us it will all be okay. Eventually, the cracks seem to stop spreading and we find a way to be content with our broken selves."

"Yes," Lias agreed, "that is how I feel now. I know I'm loved and supported, but I am still very much cracked." He asked, "How do I get better?"

"You have to finish breaking first," Celia replied. "That shattered window will never be as beautiful as it was before. No amount of tape or glue will make it last forever. Someone needs to take a crowbar and knock out all the glass from the frame. Every single shard. Then a new piece of glass can be fitted and glued in place and the light will shine through as bright as ever."

"So basically," Lias queried, "I have to be replaced with someone else to be fixed?"

"No, honey," Celia assured him. "I said you were a window, not that you were the glass. A window has many parts: a frame, a ledge, a lock, a seal, glass, and everything that holds it all together. When part of you is damaged beyond repair, you must finish breaking it in order to replace it."

"But how am I supposed to finish breaking… my dead husband?" Lias asked, tears in his eyes as he regretted his choice of words.

Celia reached out and held his hand comfortingly. "You don't break him, sweetheart. You finish breaking you. I'm sure as soon as he passed, you started to avoid thinking about him, rush through conversations where people asked about him, and avoid looking too long at things that reminded you of him."

"Yes," Lias conceded, feeling a new sense of guilt for doing so.

"But to finish breaking you," Celia continued, "you must face that hurt. Remember everything, talk about everything. The pain will be awful, but at some point, it stops being numbing when you think of him or see things that remind you of him."

Lias looked into her eyes, letting his held-back tears flow as her words sunk in.

"Now I told you that once that glass is broken, it has to be replaced. But that does not mean it is replaced exactly. The glass will never be the broken piece again. It will be a new piece, a new part of you. When you are done breaking all the little pieces of your past self with him, you can replace your glass. You will never replace his importance in your life, just his role in your life. He will never again be the man you walk hand in hand with down the street or cuddle up with at night.

He can now be a source of strength. He can be an inspiration. He can be the reason you get up each day. To take the breaths he no longer can, to hug the friends he no longer can. What that looks like depends on you, my dear. But you have to finish breaking before you can put yourself together again, and I think you still have a lot of breaking left to do."

TWENTY-TWO

Lias stared in silence at his new friend. In a matter of moments, she had managed to get to know him, assess him, love him, and provide him with wise counsel. Her words sounded like a bell ringing around him. She gave him an outlook he hadn't considered, but the moment she spoke, he knew it to be true: he had to finish breaking before he could heal.

A whoosh of air startled him as the city bus lowered its steps for passengers. Celia rose, grabbed her purse, and hugged Lias, who was now overwhelmed.

"Don't worry, honey. You'll get through this and be just fine," she whispered in his ear as they embraced. She smiled at him, then stepped away.

"Thank you," Lias replied, still puzzled by the ease with which he had connected with a complete stranger.

As the bus drove off and Lias waved goodbye, he saw Tavia jogging towards him in the distance.

"Are you done resting?" she asked when she finally reached him.

"Yes," Lias answered with conviction. "I'm done resting and ready to break."

Tavia was puzzled by his statement, but before she could ask him what he meant, he started jogging back to his apartment. She quickly followed, planning to question him later.

* * *

"See you later," Lias said as he embraced Tavia. After she left, he shut the door and welcomed the solitude.

His next task was one he preferred to do alone. He began in the kitchen, closest to the door.

The creaky cabinet yielded a black mug, pushed to the very back and concealed behind other items. It was Jonah's favorite coffee mug, too large for a beverage but he would fill it to the brim for sipping as he wrote.

Lias' hand quavered as he retrieved the mug and set it back on the counter. His eyes welled up as he remembered. He inhaled deeply and forced himself to remember: *finish breaking*.

It had been weeks since Jonah passed, and Lias had quickly hidden the mug away after the services. Today, seeing it was just as painful, but he was determined to follow the advice of the stranger he'd met earlier: it will get better and easier each day.

He proceeded to the living room, a small space with a leather couch, two end tables, and a well-used TV stand. Lias opened the doors below the stand and pulled out three pictures, stashed away weeks ago.

The first was of two twelve-year-old boys dressed in their scout uniforms, standing in front of the never-ending lake as the sun rose. Lias could still feel the humidity of that blazing day at Black Creek Scout Reservation. He ran his fingers over the photo, recalling the sense of comfort standing next to Jonah, despite his lack of enthusiasm for the activity. They smiled fiercely, with a lifetime of memories still to come.

Tears streamed down his cheeks as he placed the picture back in its home on the left side of the TV stand. Three dust-covered spaces on the stand indicated where photos used to live.

The second photo featured two newly graduated high school boys in caps and gowns standing in front of the campus fountain, hours after the ceremony ended. Lias remembered Jonah making them wait for hours while the courtyard cleared out and other graduates hurried off to prepare for the night's parties; he was captivated by the fountain and wanted a picture of them standing in front of the school, without anyone else in the frame.

Lias placed the photo on the right side of the entertainment center and a wave of emotion rushed through him. He rushed to the bathroom, barely making it to the toilet before his breakfast came up in an eruption.

The morning run and all these memories were too much for Lias to bear. Every time he allowed himself to think of his lost love for too long, his guts would explode in agony. Despite his attempts to avoid it, this was something that occurred daily. Everywhere he looked, reminders of his love surrounded him. He couldn't hide away the entire apartment, nor could he store away the memories held within his broken heart.

Celia's words echoed in his mind: "Finish breaking." Stopping now would only prolong the pain. He knew he had to keep going.

Before leaving the bathroom, Lias retrieved the monogrammed hand towels that had been tossed into the linen closet. Eternity had taken such care to select the perfect colors to match the bathroom, and the monogramming was beautiful. But as soon as Lias tried to dry his hands that first day, washing the smell of hospital and death off them, he could no longer stand to see them hanging there. The towels reminded Lias that he was alone again.

He quickly walked out of the bathroom, not allowing himself to dwell on them for now. Yet, they were still in place, and he would be forced to face them every time he went in there, which lately seemed to happen every five minutes. For now, they hung, waiting to break him even further later in the day.

As he closed the bathroom door, another closed door captured his attention. The bedroom sat in wait behind this door. It was the only room Lias had been unable to force himself into for more than a few moments at a time since Jonah's passing. The clothes he cycled through most of the time now all lived in a crumpled pile on his love seat. Determined to move forward, Lias forced himself to cross the threshold of this shrine.

The aroma of blue fern citrus air freshener hit him like a truck, bringing back memories of Jonah. Lias had been permitted to pick the fragrances for every other room of the house, but these scents were Jonah's favorites and he loved to wake up to them every day.

Closing his eyes and taking in the scents, Lias could feel Jonah still in the room. Two new canvas pictures were recently hung above the bed. One was a recreated picture of Jonah's proposal that he had convinced Matswell to take the following day at the same time. Lias recalled the irritation he felt when Jonah made them wear the same clothes as the day before. He wanted an opportunity to look better put together for the photo, but Jonah wanted to remember it just as it happened.

The second canvas was of a shocked Jonah with a face full of wedding cake, which Lias had just attacked him with. It was a sort of revenge photo on Lias' part for not being able to change clothes for the proposal photo. Matswell was in the know and a happy accomplice, ready to capture this moment well in advance.

The two recent memories and the strong smell lingering in the room burned Lias to the core. Tears escaped his swollen eyes and he stepped backward into the hall. Before he could finish putting the apartment back together and allow himself to crash, he still had one remaining photo to put back up in the living room.

The last photo now lay face down on the floor where he had dropped it before bolting out of the room to be sick. *Please don't be cracked,* Lias thought. The only thing more painful now than putting the photo back on display would be having to go out and buy a new frame before he could do that.

Luck was on his side and the frame and glass remained flawless. *You are a survivor, aren't you?* Lias reminisced on the life of the photo…

After high school graduation, Lias dragged Jonah on a week-long retreat of outdoor activities. The last activity on the last day was white-water rafting.

Desperate to capture the adventure, Jonah tried to hold steady a selfie stick up in the air off the back of the raft with one arm and his other arm wrapped around Lias, with the biggest grin on his face.

Jonah's timing was horrible as always. The moment he tried to capture was just a matter of yards from a drop. As soon as he snapped the picture, the raft jostled, and the camera and selfie stick fell into the rapids.

Desperate, Jonah searched for hours for the camera, unwilling to give up the documentation of the moment. Eventually, his determination paid off and he found the water-drenched camera. By some grace of

God, every photo on the memory card was ruined except for the one Lias now held.

The photo turned out perfect. The two boys stood at the back of the boat, and as the picture was taken, the front of the boat tipped down into a rapid, shoving everyone else onto the floor of the raft. The picture made it look like it was just the two lovers alone in the air-filled boat with a mighty rapid just behind them.

This picture lived in the middle of the entertainment center. It captured everything that Lias loved: the adventures that Jonah would allow himself to be dragged along to, the obvious love Jonah had for him, and the perseverance Jonah had for capturing moments together. That is why this was the first picture to be hidden away once Jonah passed. It was too hard to look at.

Lias' trembling hands struggled to place the photo back on the shelf. He released it and the shaking reverberated through his body, eliciting gut-wrenching, moaning sobs that soaked the carpet beneath him. He curled into a ball, his arms hugging his knees close to his chest. Before him were the three pictures that taunted him with the loving past he once shared with Jonah, reminding him painfully that there would be no more moments to capture in time.

TWENTY-THREE

Afternoon sunlight blazed down on Lias' unprotected back as he attempted to shield himself from the heat seeping through the undrawn shade. Lias sat at his desk staring at his tear-away calendar trying to remember how many days he forgot to tear away.

Suddenly, a loud slamming of the front door was followed by an annoying voice echoing down the hallway. "Rise and shine!"

Lias groaned. "What are you doing here? I gave you that key for emergencies only."

"Well, when your self-sabotaging, pain-in-the-ass little brother stops responding to his family's calls, I consider that an emergency," Eternity snapped, her gaze scanning his living quarters.

"I do answer, most of them at least," Lias corrected, pulling down his A-framed t-shirt to cover his bloated stomach.

"Look at this place," Eternity continued, her eyes widening with disgust as she kicked her way through piles of trash and dirty clothes. "This place is not fine, and neither are you. I've never seen you in such poor shape."

"This place is just fine, thank you very much," Lias retorted, though his voice lacked conviction.

"This place is not fine," she argued. "And you are not fine. Look at you. I have never seen you in such poor shape."

"It is a process. I am break—" Lias tried to say but was cut off by Eternity.

"Yeah, yeah. I heard all about your breaking. Look around, little brother. Look at yourself. You are as broken as you can be. There isn't anything left to break in this room. It is time to start healing."

Lias was silent. He had never considered this. He had not inferred that his breaking was complete.

"Looks like you have done nothing for the last few weeks but eat and sleep," Eternity accused.

"Well, you are wrong there," Lias corrected. "I have also done a fair amount of throwing up too. So there. In case you forgot, I recently lost my husband and best friend."

"We are all aware of your loss." Eternity spoke quietly. "It is no surprise that you are struggling to get back to normal."

"I don't have the energy to get back to normal," Lias admitted, his head bowed in shame.

"There is no shame in that," Eternity said softly, her hand lifting his chin so he could look into her eyes. "That is why I am here. I think you might benefit from a little medical help."

"Like liposuction?" Lias asked, a hint of hope in his voice.

"Like antidepressants. I suspect that, with everything that has happened, your hormone levels are way out of whack. If I'm right, and I usually am, then it can be near impossible for you to overcome this without help."

Lias looked around the room, his gaze eventually landing on a mirror across from him. He stood up and slowly walked towards it, examining himself closely for the first time in a month.

"I guess you're right," he near whispered.

"Of course I am," Eternity corrected. "I just need to take some blood to see what your hormone levels are, so I can get you the correct dose of antidepressants that will help you."

"Is that absolutely necessary?" Lias asked, instinctively grabbing his right arm with his left in a protective motion.

"Yes," Eternity answered. "If I get the dosage wrong, the medication can do more harm than good. And I think we can both agree that is something we need to avoid." She stood beside him, looking at the out-of-shape mess he had become in the mirror.

Lias watched as Eternity prepared to take a sample of his blood. He felt the all-too-familiar feeling of nausea, and he took off towards the bathroom as Eternity carefully put away her sample in the small black supply bag she often carried when making home visits to friends or family.

"Hormone levels being off can cause weight gain, fatigue, and nausea. I think the faster we get your results, the sooner we can get you back to normal," Eternity yelled behind him.

Lias could not lift his head from the toilet to answer her. He waved her off between bouts of vomit. She let herself out the same way that she had let herself in earlier.

As she left, Lias remembered Celia and how put together she was. Now that he agreed that he was fully broken, it was time for him to become just as put together. After having his blood drawn, Lias knew that he was ready to start healing.

The scalding water felt like a soothing balm on his skin, rejuvenating his aching muscles. He reached for his razor, determined to start taking better care of himself again. As he ran his fingers through his matted curls, the pain in his scalp reminded him of the weeks he had spent neglecting his body. He washed and conditioned his hair over, and over until he had some of his energy back.

Looking down at his newly acquired dad bod, Lias sighed. Today would be the start of his change. It was Saturday, a day that used to be part of his routine. He called his dads to see if they wanted to meet him for brunch. After that, he would go visit Vivian. He hadn't seen her in weeks, and he was worried about the effects the loneliness had had on her already fragile state.

He rummaged through his closet, but nothing fit. He had to resort to stealing some of Jonah's clothes. Lias chose a pair of relaxed-fit jeans, a comfy well-worn tee shirt, and a pair of leather sandals. Jonah's wardrobe was quite different from those of his physique. While most men built like Jonah would have firm-fitting clothes to show off their bodies, Jonah preferred clothes that brought comfort to him. Less restricting, which he found allowed ideas to flow more easily throughout him.

As Lias slid his foot into the sandal, he cursed. "The sooner Eternity fixes my hormones, the better. I can't even wear my own shoes." He was ready to go, but he couldn't help but wonder what the others thought of his casual dress code. He shook his head, knowing he was too excited about the prospect of real food to worry about it.

* * *

"Thank you," Lias smiled as their waitress set down a plate loaded with delicious Southern staples.

"You're welcome, honey," the young red-haired waitress answered, her eyes twinkling. "If you need anything else, just holler out, okay?"

"Will do," his fathers agreed in unison as the server turned to leave.

The aromas were so tantalizing that the plate hardly hit the table before Lias began shoveling mounds of food into his mouth.

"Haven't seen you eat like that since your wrestling year," Matthew chuckled.

Lias didn't pause to answer; he simply nodded as he chewed, his cheeks puffing out.

"How are you holding up?" Matthew asked, the concern evident in his voice.

"I'm all right," Lias muttered, a few crumbs popping out of his mouth as he spoke.

"I highly doubt that," Samuel interjected, his tone switching the conversation's focus. "You must be going through an unbearable nightmare. I don't understand why you insist on going through it all by yourself."

Lias took a large gulp of orange juice before replying, now that his hunger had been sated. "I'm an adult. Going through things is just part of it."

"Going through things is part of life, yes," Matthew corrected, "but there's no need to go through it all alone. That's one of the most important benefits of having family—you have people to lean on when things don't go as planned. What your dad is trying to say is that he really wants to help you more than you're allowing him to."

The three shared a moment of silence as Lias' gaze roamed between his parents, then around the room, before he spoke.

"I don't know how to let anyone help," he confessed, his eyes dropping to the ground.

"Of course you don't," Samuel echoed, reaching across the table to brush his thumb gently along Lias' cheek. "You haven't had to deal with a lot of pain in your life, and I'm so grateful for that. But since you haven't had it to deal with, we haven't had it to teach you how to manage. Why don't you come home for a while? You don't need to stay in that apartment all by yourself."

"I can't," Lias began to reply from instinct. As the words tried to form in his throat, he realized that he not only could come home, but the idea of being home warmed a part of him that he hadn't known was cold. "I'll pack a bag and come home for a bit," he said, his voice soft. "Nothing permanent. But it would be nice to be home for a while."

TWENTY-FOUR

After brunch, Lias packed a duffle bag as promised, and made his way to the nursing home to spend some much-needed time with his mother-in-law, Vivian. Waddling more than walking, Lias arrived at the home, his bag overflowing with home-cooked country treats.

Vivian was sitting in her favorite creaky rocking chair, her gaze fixed on the bright window in the corner of her room. Lias placed his bag by the foot of her bed, then took a second wooden chair across the room and sat down.

"Lias, my dear," Vivian said with a warm smile.

"Hi, Viv," he replied softly, leaning in to hug her and kiss her cheek.

"With all the family changes, I was starting to think you'd forgotten all about me," she said as she settled back into her chair.

Of course, Lias thought. *The fast wedding, the honeymoon, the funeral—so many family changes had happened so quickly. Then, after it all, Vivian had been left here to process and understand it all alone. As if she hadn't already had enough difficulties with reality. Jonah would be heartbroken if he knew I had allowed this to happen.*

"I am so sorry," Lias said, forcing himself to look at her even though he really wanted to make a mad dash for the door.

"Nonsense," Vivian waved off his apology. "You've got bigger things to worry about than little old me."

When she had these more observant moments, it was hard to remember her struggles, Lias thought. *She saw me put down the duffle bag and obviously knew that it meant I would be going home after everything that had happened.*

"You don't miss a thing, do you?" Lias asked, smirking.

"You don't get to my age without recognizing a few signs here and there, honey," Vivian replied.

"That you don't," Lias agreed.

A knock on the open door of her room drew both Lias' and Vivian's attention. A thin, sweet nurse entered, bringing a tray of food for Vivian's lunch. She set the tray down on a bedside table before wheeling it up to where Vivian sat.

"I ordered the veal shank," Vivian said, confusion evident on her face.

"I know you did," the sweet-faced young nurse said. "But with the mad rush of orders, the kitchen ran out of everything but Salisbury steak, potatoes, and vegetables. As an apology, the chef has sent you a personally-made brownie—the best this side of the Mississippi."

"I think your chef is out of practice," Vivian challenged, picking up the dessert. "I've seen more appealing brownies from a box of Little Debbie. It's not your fault, dear, but I want to speak to your manager about this. I expect more from a restaurant of this caliber."

Lias waved off the nurse as he turned to defuse the situation. He retrieved a dark hat from his bag, draping a tee shirt over his forearm like a dish towel, and lowered his voice as he began to speak to Vivian. "I am the manager, ma'am, and I am certainly sorry that the kitchen has provided you with such poor service today. I want to offer you my sincerest apologies. Your meal has been comped and I hope you will let us make it up to you for dinner tonight—also on the house, of course."

Lias felt bad for creating a confusing scene for Vivian. He was used to playing alongside her visions of who he was in the world, but never initiating the ruse.

"Will the veal be available tonight then?" Vivian asked, falling for his deception. "If I decide, that is, to give this establishment another chance."

"Of course. I wouldn't dare disappoint our most distinguished guest for two meals in a row." Lias stood, bowing before her. "Please allow me to make a call to ensure the kitchen will be better prepared for dinner."

Lias stepped out into the hallway and called his dad Samuel to figure out where he could find a last-minute lamb shank for dinner at such short notice for Vivian. Samuel agreed to take care of the situation and personally drop the meal off to Vivian on his way home from errands this evening.

Lias hung up the phone and moved back into the room, ready to announce that his kitchen staff would have her meal ready for dinner as requested. But before he had a chance to say a word, Lias noticed that in the time he had been outside her room, Vivian had hunched over in her chair, nearly burrowing her face into her waist.

"What's wrong?" Lias asked quickly, taking a knee next to her chair and tossing his costume aside before reaching out to touch her arm.

Vivian's violent sobs filled the air as they echoed through the cupped hands that surrounded her wrinkled face. Unintelligible words escaped her lips as Lias called to her, "Vivian, what's wrong?"

At the sound of his voice, Vivian let out an anguished wail, "Bryan! There is so much blood, so much blood!" Lias was used to her not recognizing him, but this time she had mistaken him for her husband. It was a role he was not prepared to play.

"Bryan!" Vivian yelled through her cupped hands. "Don't just sit there like a fool, do something!"

Lias froze, his mouth open in shock. In a voice so quiet he could barely hear himself, he asked, "What should I do?" Vivian's demand hung in the air and all Lias could do was wait for an answer.

"They're going to die if we do nothing," Vivian roared at him.

Suddenly, the sweet nurse from earlier entered the room with a needle meant to relax Vivian. Vivian continued to scream, her eyes never leaving Lias, until the nurse injected her. Within seconds, Vivian went completely silent and closed her eyes.

"Help me lay her down, will you?" the nurse asked Lias, who had already risen to his feet.

"I've never seen her get like that before," Lias said in a tone of questioning disbelief.

"Sadly, it's become a regular occurrence," the nurse said softly as they gently laid Vivian in her bed. "It started a few months ago, but recently it's almost daily."

"Has she mentioned who she's worried about?" Lias asked. "Maybe I could bring that person here to see her and it will help calm her."

"No," the nurse answered. "She never mentions anyone's name that I have heard. At her age, we can't leave her in that state for too long. She could hurt herself being so upset. She might not even know who she believes is in need of help."

Lias' heart sank as he realized that the timing of Vivian's panic attacks coincided with the time when Jonah stopped visiting her regularly. *She's frightened and alone*, he thought. *Here I am, at home with a family full of people willing to help me, and I refuse to let them, while Vivian is here alone and needs that support.*

"I'll make it a point to be around more often," Lias promised. "I'm sure she's feeling trapped and alone with no one coming to see her regularly."

"I think that will be great for her," the helpful nurse said as she left the room, her gaze already set down the hall to her next patient.

TWENTY-FIVE

Lias stared at the ceiling of his childhood bedroom, replaying the afternoon with Vivian in his mind. Regret filled him as he remembered how he had all but forgotten about his mother-in-law amidst his own grief. He was reminded of the pain Vivian must have endured daily for months: the pain of losing the last family she had in the world.

A familiar churning in his stomach signaled to Lias that he had only seconds to make it to the bathroom before he would have to vomit. Thankfully, his father had foreseen the need for a shared bathroom in the boys' bedroom.

As Lias flushed the toilet, Eternity's voice startled him. "I was right. Your hormone levels are extremely off. Your estrogen levels are through the roof."

Confused, Lias asked, "How can that be?"

"Our bodies all react differently to stress," Eternity explained. "With all that you've been through, your body seems to have forgotten how to properly balance estrogen. Stress can naturally raise your estrogen levels, and then how you handle that stress—such as stress eating—can add to it. Certain herbs can also increase your estrogen levels, like ginseng and ginkgo. Who knows what herbs were used when preparing the food you had on your honeymoon."

"There was quite a variety," Lias remembered. "So, all of this is related to my estrogen levels?"

"Yes," Eternity confirmed. "Fatigue, weight gain, mood swings, and even puffiness can all be influenced by this."

"Puffiness?!" Lias exclaimed. "I didn't mention that."

"No, you didn't," Eternity agreed. "But the fact that you haven't had a pair of real shoes on your feet for weeks tells me that you're having trouble fitting into them due to puffiness."

Lias huffed, and a tear escaped down his face. He had already noticed the changes in his appearance from his recent overeating. But he had not allowed himself to consider puffiness as a potential symptom.

"So," he spoke, wiping away his tears. "What do we do about it?"

"Nothing too complicated," Eternity reassured him. "A better diet, no more junk food for a while, more exercise, more water, and some medication to help you along the way.

"How long will it take for me to get better?" Lias asked.

"It can vary," Eternity replied. "But if you make a solid effort, you should start to see improvements in a few weeks."

Lias echoed her words, "A few weeks."

"Hey, this didn't happen to you overnight, and nothing is going to fix it overnight," Eternity reminded him.

It sure felt like it happened overnight, Lias thought. *One minute I am celebrating my wedding, and the next minute it hurts to move.*

"I have to get back to the hospital," Eternity said as she threw a small bottle of pills at Lias. "I have surgery in an hour."

"Thanks," Lias replied, watching as his sister walked out of the room and down the hallway.

It's time for me to get back to my old self, he thought. *Jonah, you know I will always love and miss you with all my heart. I'm going to take better care of Vivian, I promise.*

Motivated by this thought, Lias decided to start with a healthier late lunch than the junk food he had been eating recently.

The kitchen at Anderson Manor was a sight to behold. Matthew had spared no expense in creating a kitchen that was both beautiful and functional. The farthest wall was three-fourths floor-to-ceiling windows that overlooked the meticulously manicured backyard. Whenever Lias looked out at the hedges surrounding the lawn, he felt a sense of serene safety.

In the center of the kitchen, an enormous double island with a white marble countertop awaited him. As he ran his hand over the smooth surface, Lias felt as though decades had passed since he'd spent much time in the kitchen.

Vivid memories of the island covered in buffet-style meals for every holiday imaginable came flooding back. This kitchen was the gathering point for friends and family to celebrate their most beloved occasions—something Lias had taken for granted until now. The restaurant-style, clear-glass double-door refrigerator was always stocked with selections more suited for a fine dining experience than a casual meal at home. Lias perused the options with the cool, frosted air of the fridge soothing his weary face.

He lingered longer than necessary, enjoying the temporary oasis. The cool breeze was doing its job, calming his clammy skin. All the food tempted his stomach, but his mind was set—he would take better care of himself.

Lias opted for a fresh salad as an appropriate lunch. He ventured down the hallway to the small indoor greenhouse of his childhood home, a relic of his Papa's youth. The flavor of love that can only be tasted in the crops planted and harvested with one's own hands called to him.

This is what Lias searched for today. He could feel the energy glowing off the produce as he made his way around the room, picking tomatoes, cucumbers, peppers, carrots, and lettuce. The homey scent coming off each as he held them close was heavenly. The earthy textures against his skin as he picked each piece carefully filled his soul.

Lias thought back to the dozens of market trips he'd taken with Jonah since they moved in together— he'd never experienced the produce calling to him like the greenery in this room did now. He never felt the vegetables hug him back the way those he now held did. Perhaps his Papa was right—there was something to his theory.

As he chopped his bounty in the kitchen, Lias eagerly anticipated the first bite of the bowl full of love that he had prepared. And a full bowl it was. *Baby steps*, he thought to himself—*a heaping bowl of salad was better than a heaping bowl of junk, right?*

He did not linger long on the thought. As the first bite hit his lips, his only concern was savoring every morsel. As he swallowed the first mouthful, a tingle washed over his skin, and a patch of bubbles churned in his stomach. This was what his body wanted; this is what he needed.

TWENTY-SIX

The sun beat down on Lias' skin as he paused his morning jog, standing in front of the infamous bus stop bench. All too easily, he remembered how just a few weeks ago he was unable to complete the jog with Tavia without having to stop and rest here.

Lias used the bottom of his shirt to wipe away the sweat and humidity from his forehead. He was relieved to finally feel some energy course through his body. Eternity had been right, he was improving.

As he finished wiping himself down, he glanced down at his still-bloated abdomen.

"I'm sure you'll be the next to go," he whispered to his stomach. "Your days are numbered."

He poked at the hard pudge and felt the muscle underneath respond, flexing from the strenuous exercise he had been forcing it to endure lately.

The hiss of air caught his attention as the bus lowered to let passengers off. Lias lingered, hoping to catch a glimpse of Celia one more time. To thank her for her kind words when he was at his lowest. To show her that he was done breaking and was finally getting his life back on track, just like she had.

As the last disgruntled man stepped off the bus and it prepared to pull away, a cramp in Lias' gut almost brought him to his knees. His tense muscles continued to push back, forcing his focus away from the hope of seeing his friend to the increasing twisting spasms that threatened to take him down.

Lias sat down on the familiar bench, bent over as he waited for the pain to pass. He realized he had been pushing his body too hard in an effort to get back in shape without realizing how far he had gone today.

His phone rang loudly as he sat, trying to alleviate the tightness in his insides. It rang for a while before he was able to muster enough of a voice to answer. "Hello."

"Finally," Eternity's annoyed voice rang through the phone. "I got the follow-up results back from your hormone tests and they're still high in estrogen. Are you taking your meds?"

"Yes," Lias replied before wincing as another wave of cramping attacked his stomach.

"Are you following the diet we talked about? Are you getting enough exercise?" Eternity asked in the way only a physician can.

"Yes," Lias answered after a moment when the cramping paused. "I'm doing everything you told me to do. I've been working out twice a day, pushing myself so hard that I'm currently stuck on this bench, unable to move because of the cramps."

"Don't push it," Eternity's voice softened. "That won't help anyone. Listen to your body, it will tell you when it's time to stop. I'll be by the house later and we'll look at changing up your meds. I suggest you call it a day for your exercise and get back home, take it easy for a bit."

"Okay," Lias said through gritted teeth, holding back a grimace.

"Okay, I'll see you later," Eternity said before someone else on the phone drew her attention away. "Get some rest till then."

She hung up before Lias could answer. He was grateful for that. He just wanted to focus on getting himself home and laying down.

The walk home seemed to take forever as he had to pause every few steps to catch his breath. *So much for progress*, he thought. Even as he walked, he could feel the sweat dripping down his body.

Though he was exhausted and could barely stand once he got home, Lias had a routine to follow if he hoped to get back to normal. *Skin care is important*, he reminded himself. *Routine through the pain or be a mess forever.*

He slathered on a thick glob of facial mud working it around with a thick brush to cover every inch of his face up to his eyes as close as possible. He tilted his head as far back as he could to keep the drying mud from dripping down his face while he mindlessly shimmied out of his shorts, before kicking the shorts across the floor into the corner. He reached for the shower knob and turned it up as high as it would go.

Stepping into the shower, he allowed the scalding water to cascade over his face and body, letting the mud trickle down his body. No longer did showers have the soothing effect he remembered from his childhood. Whenever water touched his skin, especially his face, his mind would take him back to

Jonah. Again and again, he would relive the worst memory of his life.

Clenching his eyes shut, he could see the circle of tormentors circling Jonah. He could feel the fear in his own heart and would watch, for the thousandth time, as Jonah's limp body flew through the sea as the tail of the beast flailed against him.

A new, familiar pain wrung his gut. The pain that the water always brought. Lias opened his tear-filled eyes and let the scalding water sting them. His already overworked body did not have the strength to remember anymore. The physical pain he felt as he turned off the now-cold water was enough to bring him back to the present.

Reaching out for his towel, he quickly dried off his body, wrapping the towel around his face to keep in the warmth, and stumbled into his bed, passing out as soon as his face hit the pillow.

The air was thick with worried voices when Lias woke up to the sound of his father calling his name, "Lias, Lias honey, wake up," Samuel pleaded.

"I am up," Lias grumbled without opening his eyes. "What's wrong?"

Samuel answered in the fast, high-pitched voice of a worried dad. "Are you okay?"

Lias opened his eyes at the familiar sound of his panicked father. "Yes, what are you so upset about?" he asked.

"I bought some new soap for your bathroom and when I went in there, I found these," Samuel squeaked, waving Lias' shorts.

"What is wrong with my shorts?" Lias asked as he sat up in bed wiping sleep from his eyes.

As he asked, Samuel turned them around and Lias could see that the back of them was covered in blood. "Did you cut yourself on something as you were exercising today?"

Deep-buried instinct took over at the mention of his blood around his father, and Lias became an impenetrable fortress. Because of the family secret Samuel often overreacted when it came to any type of injury with one of his children.

Lias recalled shortly after turning six when the family temporarily moved back to his father's hometown in Nebraska getting a pretty substantial, for a six-year-old, cut jumping over a pile of yard debris when a sharp stick dug into his leg. Samuel did not permit Lias to return to school for nearly two weeks until the last of the scab fell.

Knowing the family secret now, Lias knew Samuel worried that even a piece of a scab that fell off and into the wrong hands could be a downfall to the family. But, having a father concerned with every minor injury created a barrier in which Lias went to any extreme to hide even the littlest of bruises from his Dad. Even with logic on his side now to know his father's intention, decades of habitually hiding injury could not be broken in a single moment.

Catching up to his father's worry, Lias tried to remain calm to soothe him. Even though the blood worried Lias as well, he knew the extreme fear that built in his father of every little thing. He would have to calm Samuel down in order to be self-worried in private. "No, I don't think I cut myself. I guess I may have overdone it with the exercise and diet." Lias spoke with a non-convincing shatter in his voice.

"This does not come from exercising," Samuel panicked, assuming where the blood must have come from if it wasn't from an accidental cut.

"Dad, this is not the first time I have bled a little," Lias continued, still attempting to reassure him while searching for a logical explanation for the excessive blood on the back of his shorts.

"This is not a little blood," Samuel corrected. "This amount of blood is not normal for anything. Something is wrong."

By now Lias was fully awake, and he realized his father was right, and there was no hope to calm him down. There was no reason for him to be bleeding, and definitely not this much.

"I am sure everything is fine," Lias tried again to be soothing. Partially for his father, but also for himself. The idea of one more thing in his life going wrong was too much for Lias to consider as he was already struggling to put his broken life back together. "Eternity said she would be here this afternoon; she can check me out if it will make you feel better."

Lias said the words intended to calm his father, but he was beginning to grow in worry himself, as he could now more clearly see the amount of blood that stained the back of his shorts.

"Could you get me some water?" Lias asked his father hoping for an unmonitored moment to wrap his mind around everything going on.

Samuel did not move at the request. He stood as still as a statue, staring at his son.

"I'm fine, Dad. Water please?" Lias asked with a begging tone.

Parental instincts took over at the sound of need in his son's voice and Samuel turned to quickly walk out of the room.

Once he had the room to himself, Lias did a quick assessment of himself, realizing that a small pool of drying blood was also between his thighs.

Some time passed and Samuel did not return. Longer than necessary to retrieve a glass of water. Lias was grateful for the time to fully inspect himself before his father returned. *Doesn't seem like I'm bleeding now*, Lias thought as he felt around himself. *No reason to stress Dad out further.*

Lias quickly threw the covers back over the evidence that he may not be as fine as he wanted his father to believe he was, just as he heard footsteps creaking down the hall.

"Here you go," Samuel held out the glass for his son to drink.

"Thanks, Dad," Lias answered. "Stop staring at me like I'm broken. I'm fine. Everything is fine. It's just a little blood."

"I'll be the judge of that," Eternity declared as she stepped into the bedroom.

TWENTY-SEVEN

Eternity gracefully moved around the homemade clinic, as though she belonged there. This was her element. Most homes had playrooms, pool tables, or storage in their basements, but the Anderson family had their own personal medical clinic. They couldn't risk going to a regular doctor, as they had a family secret they wanted to keep hidden.

Lias was growing bored of his sister's prodding and probing. He continued trying to convince himself that this was an exaggerated reaction to the little bit of blood. He thought to himself, *it's not that bad and I'm obviously fine*. He was just as unconvincing with himself as he had been with his father and sister. He knew something was wrong. Even before today, Lias had felt for a while that something was wrong with him.

The right wall of the exam table he was sitting on was lined with cabinets filled with various medical supplies, and above them were sterile countertops.

To his left, computer monitors hung from the wall, along with some portable medical devices. The clinic's inventory had grown over the years from when the children were younger. Back then, the only medical supplies were a blood pressure cuff, a thermometer, and a microscope. Fortunately, none of the kids had ever required anything more than a few band-aids or a cup of soup. It was a miracle, considering how reckless Lias could be with his decisions.

Since Eternity, a formally trained doctor and surgeon, had taken over the clinic, their basement could easily rival that of many third-world medical facilities. She had begun to search through the cabinets, although Lias couldn't tell what she was looking for.

Lias just wanted her to give his dad a clean bill of health so that he would stop worrying. As usual, Samuel was asked to wait in the upstairs room. His overprotectiveness and hypochondria weren't very helpful to anyone who entered the clinic. As soon as Samuel was gone from the reason Lias could now focus solely on trying to make himself believe that he was okay. *Manifest it*, he thought. *Manifest it.*

Since Eternity was the oldest child and a familiar caregiver to Lias, he felt as comfortable as possible while she poked, prodded, and took swabs from various regions. Ever since puberty, Lias and Matswell had both been grateful for the private doctor who was aware of the changes they were going through. Neither wanted to have to talk to Matthew about the physical changes they were going through.

The cool air of the basement, and the fact that Eternity had taken a break from her duties, caused Lias to lean back and relax. As he closed his eyes, the sound of gushing waves surrounded him. The familiar sensation of water rocking the boat beneath his feet shocked him, and he opened his eyes.

He was aware that he was dreaming but didn't care. A few feet across the boat in front of him, Jonah was sitting quietly writing. Of the thousands of Jonah-related dreams he had struggled through in the last months, rarely were any of them peaceful and calm.

This was a moment Lias remembered well; snacking, and watching Jonah write as they sailed. This was the last peaceful memory they had together, and he was thankful to be able to relive it.

"What are you writing?" Lias asked the memory of Jonah, something he wished he had asked at the moment. Amidst all the chaos of the incident, he hadn't thought to try and recover the makeshift journal that his husband was writing in.

"Everything," Jonah turned his head to the side over his shoulder to answer. "There is so much beauty out here, I don't want to forget a single moment of this."

This was a typical response from Jonah. He always found something to appreciate in every interaction. That was the writer in him. Even a trip to the mailbox could turn into an epic story of a hero overcoming storms and saving a parcel that would save the world from evil's peril.

Jonah's optimism was what Lias had missed the most. Lias walked over to his husband, hoping to hug him one last time. As he got close, the boat rocked, and a massive torrent of cold water splashed his shirt. Instinctively, he began to try and take it off, but it seemed to be stuck to his skin.

"It's so cold," Lias told Jonah as he struggled to free himself from his shirt.

In an effort to warm his partner up and dry the water, Jonah began to fan at Lias with the journal he was writing in. The fanning only made the water feel colder against his skin, as the notebook passed over his stomach.

"What is it?" a familiar voice boomed from nowhere.

Lias looked around the boat for the source of the voice. His father, Matthew, was nowhere to be found, but his voice seemed to be coming from the sea.

"It's bad," Eternity's sharp voice joined in from the sky.

As Lias spun around in a circle, looking for the source of the voices, the scene changed. When he completed his 360, Jonah was no longer there. Looking out over the sides of the *Driftwood*, the perfectly clear blue tint of the waters had darkened to a weary crimson as he turned.

"How bad?" The waves darkened even more, as Matthew's voice continued to fill the emptiness around the boat. "What do we do?"

"Emergency surgery today," Eternity's voice caused lightning strikes from the sky to crash into the darkened waves. "I'll be back soon. Get him ready."

Lias tried to wake up and find out what the sky and the sea had been arguing about, but he couldn't get his eyes to open. He stood still, as the waves of bloody sea sloshed at his feet, pleading, unsuccessfully, with himself to wake up.

"Where? How?" the sea roared.

"Here," the sky mocked. "This is what this place was designed for."

"I know, I designed it," the sea hissed, thrashing even harder. "But making it this far, barely used, I have become content with it collecting dust."

The splashing bloody waves thrashed harder and louder against Lias, drowning out the conversation until he could no longer make out what it meant. A final mighty splash assaulted the boat, causing Lias to lose his footing, and everything went dark.

TWENTY-EIGHT

s **his** foggy eyes attempted to focus in the brilliantly lit room, Lias attempted to make sense of everything that had happened: his last conversation with his father, the strange dream, *or warning*. He could discern the familiar yet confusing voices of his father and sister in the background.

The creaking of a worn metal chair behind him caused Lias' heart to race.

"I apologize," Matthew's voice wavered. "I didn't mean to startle you. Are you feeling all right?"

Lias inhaled deeply, realizing it was only his Papa. Lias knew he was expected to answer, but his brain felt cloudy, and it was difficult to concentrate. "Sorry, what did you say?" he finally asked, gazing into his father's anxious eyes.

"I asked if you were feeling all right," Matthew repeated.

"I'm confused," Lias admitted. "What's going on?"

As he asked the question, Lias noticed some changes in the room. It was far brighter than he recalled it being. All the times he snuck down here to play as a kid, the room had never been as illuminated as it was now. There was no way for any of the dark shadows he remembered scaring him as a child to hide.

"I imagine you are," Matthew said. "There's a lot for you to learn that came to light in just a short period of time."

Lias slowly stood up with some difficulty, waving off his Papa who quickly rose to try and help him.

"I can sense that," Lias said, staring at the light shining down on him.

"Yes, I imagine you can," Matthew agreed. "After finding your blood-soaked shorts, your father called Eternity."

"I know," Lias interjected, but went quiet as his Papa's eyes verified what his intuition was telling him now—there was much more to discover.

"Well," Matthew cleared his throat, "it's a good thing he did. By the time I had gotten home, Eternity had already conducted a few tests to find out what was causing you to bleed so much. As it turns out, she found a mass growing in your abdomen."

Lias instinctively put his hand on his stomach as his father spoke. "That explains the gut I can't seem to get rid of no matter what I do."

"Without actually taking you to a hospital and exposing you to outsiders testing your body..." Matthew kept talking, but Lias' mind had already wandered. He knew that a hospital visit was out of the question. His and his siblings' special DNA—DNA formed from both his fathers—was not public knowledge. The family secret was the reason for the overwhelmingly bright room he now sat in.

Growing up, Matthew had managed the minor traumas. But nothing further than what an ice pack and an ace bandage could treat was ever needed. He was a biologist, not a doctor. As soon as Eternity had finished medical school, she took over this home clinic.

"Surgery," Matthew said, bringing Lias' attention back. "Eternity feels that the best course of action is to remove the mass as soon as possible before it causes any further damage."

Lias nodded to indicate that he had heard his father's words as he continued to examine the room with a newfound understanding.

Matthew asked, "Where is she?"

"She went out to get supplies we don't have here," Matthew replied with a quivering voice, trying to make a joke out of it. "I mean, I can't exactly keep blood stocked here."

Lias tried to alleviate his father's worry. "It's okay, Papa. Eternity is great at her job. If she thinks this will help, then it will help."

Matthew stared into his son's eyes, amazed at his courage. "Does nothing phase you? I just told you that you're hours away from surgery and seconds later you're trying to comfort me."

Lias nodded. "Of course it does. But I can feel that something has been wrong with my body for a while now. It's like every system of my body has been off. Knowing that Eternity can solve it is such a relief."

Matthew regarded his son in admiration.

"Honestly, it's exciting to know that after this I can get back to my old self," Lias said.

Just then, Eternity walked in, followed by Tavia. With a frame in hand, she hung a transparent image of the mass on the wall and flipped a switch to light it up.

"Here is the mass," Eternity said, pointing to the lower portion of the image. Lias, Tavia, and Matthew, all studied it as Eternity talked through its positioning and how important it was to remove it quickly to avoid further complications.

"Why does it say M. Taylor?" Lias asked.

"Well, I can't exactly put your name on it and risk anyone asking questions, now can I?" Eternity replied.

Lias nodded in understanding. His thoughts still felt foggy, but he knew that she had to use a pseudonym to get it.

"We need to get you ready as soon as possible," Eternity said, looking at her brother but speaking to their father. "I have my shifts covered at the hospital for the next few days to make sure I'm here through your recovery."

Lias agreed, "Let's get me ready for surgery."

TWENTY-NINE

As **Lias** prepared for his upcoming surgery, he spoke to each of his sisters and his father. Matswell left for work shortly after Jonah's funeral.

Samuel had to drag Matthew upstairs, as he was adamant about being a part of the procedure, despite

Eternity's insistence that it would be too emotionally taxing.

After a heated debate, Lias asked Tavia to stand in for Matthew, as they had always shared a strong bond. He knew that if anyone could push down their feelings and be of assistance, it would be her.

Matthew hated feeling powerless, but he trusted his daughter's judgment and allowed Samuel to take him away. He placed all his faith in his children: Lias to be brave and strong, Eternity to be precise and accurate, and Tavia to be the rock that she always was for the family.

As the room quieted, Lias felt his heartbeat thumping in the machine attached to his finger. He took deep breaths, trying to remain composed in front of his family, though something deep inside him told him he should be worried, that he should get up and run. The irrational thought that he had any cause for fear after his accomplished sister surgeon's reassurances did nothing to calm him.

Run from what? He thought. *Run from my loving sister who is trying to cure me?* The illogical thought that in any way he had anything to fear now after all the accolades from his highly qualified sister surgeon did not help calm him.

"It's normal to be nervous," Eternity said, her voice shaking. "I have done hundreds of surgeries. I can do this."

"I know," Lias replied, grasping her hand. "I'm not worried about you, I'm worried about me. The past few months have been an emotional rollercoaster and I'm still a bit shaken up from it."

"It's almost over," Eternity said, her voice breaking again. She cleared her throat and tried to reassure him. "Everything will be fixed soon, I promise."

Eternity handed his hand to Tavia, tilting her head back to prevent a tear from escaping, "I need to get the anesthesia ready. We should get going."

Lias closed his eyes and bowed his head, fear and apprehension coursing through him.

"Don't be afraid," Tavia said, her voice laced with humor. "Lots of people would love to have this surgery and have instant weight loss!"

Lias smiled, still not opening his eyes. "Lucky me," he whispered.

"Lucky you," Tavia agreed.

Eternity stepped forward with a long tube and triangular cup. As she placed it over Lias' nose, she asked him to count backward from ten.

"Ten, nine, eight, seven, si..." Lias trailed off as the anesthesia kicked in.

"Let's get going," Eternity declared, wheeling the ultrasound machine from across the room.

"What's that for?" Tavia asked.

"I need to make sure nothing has changed or moved before I start," Eternity replied.

Tavia glanced around the room, memories flooding her mind. She remembered the times she would grip Lias' tiny hand tightly when they were at the zoo to keep him from running away. Before the anesthesia kicked in it felt like she was keeping him from running again.

Eternity dropped the lubed hose of the ultrasound machine, the clang of metal against metal snapping Tavia back to the present.

"Sorry," Eternity said automatically.

Tavia didn't respond, only watched Eternity's movements. She was used to seeing her sister act with precision in all she did, but preparing to operate on her baby brother was clearly taking a toll on her.

Eternity closed her eyes and paused, obviously centering herself before beginning. Tavia stayed still and silent, allowing her sister that moment of privacy. After a few moments, Eternity opened her eyes and picked up the attachment again. This time, Tavia was sure she saw a glimmer of a tear in her sister's eye.

Tavia watched as Eternity rolled the sticky gel-covered wand over Lias' abdomen and marked the skin with a marker. *A road map for the incision*, Tavia thought, her stomach churning. She quickly looked away from her brother and toward the screen, silently telling herself to stay strong. She stared at the out-of-focus waves on the screen as Eternity moved the machine across Lias. She couldn't bring herself to look down at him.

After a few moments, her military training kicked in and she scolded herself. *Chin up and do what needs to be done.* She turned to look at her brother and, though the sight was overwhelming, she kept her focus across the room, looking for a distraction.

Her gaze landed on the transparent sheet Eternity hung earlier, showing the family what was going on inside Lias. She imagined the lump, which was known as M. Taylor, as a miniature Nerf ball.

Eternity finished the pre-surgery marks and Tavia snapped her head back to the ultrasound machine. The image of the near perfect circle shape burned in her mind as Eternity reached for the scalpel. The soldier in Tavia couldn't watch and quickly looked back at the M. Taylor image.

The oblong image was the same shape as she remembered, though it wasn't the same as the one that appeared on the ultrasound. As Tavia tried to remember the image, adrenaline coursed through her veins. Her body knew something her brain hadn't connected yet.

"Stop!" she shouted as it clicked, her realization improbable.

Eternity steadied her left hand on the operating table and pulled the blade against Lias' skin, taking a steadying breath.

"What?" Eternity squeaked, not wavering the scalpel against her brother's skin.

"Get that blade away from him," Tavia commanded, her voice steady like a commander before a battle.

Eternity stopped, but the scalpel remained just centimeters from Lias' abdomen.

"It is not a mass," Tavia said, her gaze meeting Eternity's and revealing something she recognized. The dark eyes that stared back at her revealed the truth. "But you already knew that, didn't you?" Tavia accused, her voice gaining an even sterner edge as she stepped purposefully toward her sister.

"It has to be done," Eternity pleaded. "It's the only way to save him."

"Get that blade away from him," Tavia commanded, "or that hand will never be fit for surgery again."

Eternity heard the sincerity in her sister's threat. While they were both strong and trained in self-defense, she knew that if Tavia's mind was set on destroying her arm, it would never be usable again. Eternity knew firsthand the devastation Tavia could cause if she wished. Tavia took a second step towards her, now arm's length away from breaking her arm.

"You don't understand," Eternity pleaded, her eyes still guilty.

"Then make me understand," Tavia countered. "After you step away from him with that blade. This is the last time I'm going to ask."

Seconds later, the sound of metal clattering on the tray as Eternity dropped the scalpel echoed off the walls of the room. Slowly, Eternity stepped back from her unconscious brother and turned her back to her sister in shame.

THIRTY

As the ringing of her sharp scalpel still echoed in the room, Eternity dragged a chair to the farthest corner of the room, away from her unconscious brother. She buried her face in her hands, her body shaking from heavy tears.

The calculated footsteps of her baby sister, Tavia, vibrated through the room as soon as the scalpel stopped ringing in Eternity's ears. Tavia paused behind her sister, standing between her sister and her brother.

"I saw what I thought I saw, didn't I?" Tavia demanded, her authoritative tone making it clear that there was only one acceptable answer.

"Yes," Eternity mumbled after a few seconds, trying to stifle her tears. "You saw what you saw."

"Then why would you do it? How could you?" Tavia's questions were laced with accusation.

"I was going to do what I had to do to keep this family together. You haven't seen what I've seen, Tavia," Eternity spat with defiance against the judgment in her sister's inquisition.

Tavia placed a firm hand on the back of her sister's chair and forced it to spin, so Eternity had to face her as they talked.

Eternity did not resist. She knew her sister well enough to understand that it would only cause more trouble.

"What you had to do?" Tavia repeated.

"Yes, what I had to do," Eternity replied slowly. "With what I know, and what I've seen it was what I felt I had to do."

Eternity took a step toward her brother. Tavia's body was boiling with blood.

"Relax," Eternity instructed. "I am unarmed. I am going to get something—also not a weapon—from my bag." Tavia stiffened.

"I said relax," Eternity repeated, though Tavia did not. Instead, she stepped back, creating a path for Eternity to her bag without allowing even the slightest access to the drugged Lias. Returning to her chair, Eternity held a manila folder in her hands. Tavia dragged a small metal chair closer, positioning it in the path of travel, effectively pinning her sister into the corner.

Eternity rummaged through some documents, eventually producing a printout of what appeared to be an ultrasound image. Softly, she asked, "What is hanging on the wall is a fake. This is the real one. What do you see?"

Tavia studied the image in her hands. "I see something I cannot explain. Against all odds, I see a baby growing inside my brother." She glanced at him before returning the image to Eternity. "I see a choice that you almost took away from him without giving him all the facts. I see betrayal. I see a life ended before it can begin."

Eternity took the image back, her voice trembling. "Before you judge me further, let me tell you what I see. I see men in dark glasses, rifling through hospital files. I see military personnel turning over furniture in this house. I see my family—in handcuffs—being taken away never to be seen again." Tears glistened in her eyes.

"I—" Tavia began, but Eternity shook her head as if to say *I'm not done*.

"We figure stuff out," Tavia said, her voice full of conviction. "We are a family. We work through things together."

Eternity nodded. "You think I came to this idea in a vacuum? Believe it or not, this isn't the first medical miracle I've seen. I've seen firsthand what happens to families like ours."

"What are you talking about?" Tavia questioned. "What have you seen?"

"Remember my sabbatical a few years ago?" Eternity asked. "The time I traveled the world?"

"Yes..."

"Yes, and no." Eternity corrected. "I was traveling but never left the US. I was searching for someone."

"Who?" Tavia was stunned. She knew her sister was capable of finding anyone with her resources yet failed to include her in the search.

"Emilia." Eternity sighed, her eyes distant. "She was a nearly fifteen-year-old patient I consulted on in Montana for an old colleague. She lived on an eighty-acre farm with her mom and seven sisters. When she was seven, she was riding a plow with her dad and got into an accident. Her dad died instantly, and she was severely injured. Miraculously, she survived, but the doctors had to remove her ovaries and both fallopian tubes."

"What does any of this have to do with our brother?" Tavia asked, feeling empathy for the poor girl.

"Emilia…" Eternity continued, "After that day, she lived with eight women and no men in the middle of nowhere. No vehicle. The closest homes were nearly a day away by horse and carriage. The children were homeschooled and never left the farm."

"Not even for medical care?" Tavia questioned.

"No. They didn't believe in modern medicine. When the plow accident occurred, one of the younger sisters called an operator for help. A medevac chopper arrived in time to save Emilia, but not her father."

Tavia was growing impatient with the story. "Yes, but I ask again: *what does this have to do with Lias now?*"

"Everything." Eternity's spat. "Seven years after the accident, Emilia's mother voluntarily brought her into the closest hospital."

"Against her beliefs?" Tavia challenged.

"Because of her beliefs." Eternity corrected. "Her mother knew the impossible signs her daughter was displaying. My former colleague was baffled to the point that he called me. Everyone who knows me is aware of my fascination with the unexplainable. What I saw when I got there was unique. This farm girl, who lived with all women, was obviously a virgin, with no ovaries, no fallopian tubes, and yet was quite pregnant."

The similarities between Emilia and Lias' stories clicked for Tavia, yet she remained unconvinced of her sister's actions.

"Medical mysteries exist, I get it," Tavia offered, "but that's not good enough reason for—"

"That was the background, not the whole story," Eternity said, her gaze locked onto her sister's. Tavia knew she had to let her finish this memory, no matter how painful it was.

"As you'd expect," Eternity continued, her voice shaking, "the news about the pregnant, unmarried farm girl spread through the small town like wildfire. And the first people to arrive with pitchforks and condemnation were a group led by the local pastor."

Tavia sat quietly, watching the pain on her sister's face as her words evoked a painful past.

"I stayed there for about a week, fascinated by the situation," Eternity admitted. "It was incredible to witness something so unexplainable with my own eyes. The day after the pastor's angry mob, an even scarier group arrived at the hospital, led by a single, unnamed doctor in a long lab coat."

A battalion of military personnel followed him, and they took Emilia and her family away. Every document, photo, and clipboard related to her was collected and destroyed. I saw the terror on the families' faces as they were dragged away by our own government."

Tavia finally understood. She had been in charge of similar operations before, and she knew that a pregnant virgin farm girl could be seen as a threat. Something that the government wasn't willing to take lightly.

"The next day, I drove out to Emilia's home in the middle of nowhere," Eternity sobbed, "and there was no sign of anyone living there anymore. When I got back to town, I searched the internet and the courthouse records, but it appeared that the family had been erased from existence. No one had known them before, so no one missed them. An entire family was gone in a day, all because of something that they couldn't explain—something that scared them."

The sisters sat in silence for a while before Eternity spoke.

"As soon as I saw what was going on with Lias on that ultrasound," she said, "I started watching my back, expecting soldiers to come and take away everything that I care about. I had to keep the secret and fix the situation myself."

"Frankly, I can't imagine the trauma and stress of living through this and keeping it to yourself," Tavia said, her voice firm. "But that doesn't give you the right to make life-changing decisions for this family on your own. We all know the risks that come with our family's taboo history. We don't know what tomorrow will bring, but we'll face it together—that's how we were raised. This situation is scary, yes, but it's also exciting! Something amazing is happening in this room right now."

Tavia glanced at her silent brother, and finally, the picture became clear. Eternity had witnessed the fear of having your secret exposed. She had seen the horror of a baby growing in her baby brother's abdomen.

"Jonah lives on," Tavia said, her voice soft.

Eternity stared at Lias in shame as her sister uttered their fallen brother's name.

"I almost ruined it all," Eternity sobbed, dropping to her knees and burying her face in her palms. A string of unintelligible words followed, but Tavia couldn't make them out.

Tavia knelt on the floor and sat behind Eternity, wrapping an awkward arm around her.

"What am I supposed to tell him?" Eternity whimpered through her tears. "He's going to hate me now."

"You're going to tell him the truth," Tavia said. "You're going to tell him that you used your medical training to make the best choice you could given the circumstances, but realized at the last minute that you were wrong. You're going to tell him that you weren't trained to look for this and had no way of knowing it was a possibility. You're going to tell him that you're heartbroken over what could have happened, but it didn't. Nothing happened. He doesn't have a scratch on him, and there's nothing he needs to know right now."

Eternity looked up from her palms. "I don't tell him the rest?"

"Is it still in your heart to harm this child?" Tavia asked, her voice full of resolve.

"No," Eternity sobbed. "I never wanted to; I just couldn't see any other way."

"Then there's nothing more that will benefit him, or anyone else, to know," Tavia said. "We also won't tell him about the millionaire I could have been if I'd bought the right ticket, or the stomachache I could have had if I'd eaten that gas station burrito."

Tavia reached out to give her sister a real hug. "What do we do now?" Eternity asked.

Tavia stood up and extended her hand to her sister. "We wake Lias, we wait for Matswell to get here, and we tell the family that we have a new secret. What happens from there is all up to Lias."

THIRTY-ONE

As the room around him filled with a cacophony of chatter that he could not comprehend, Lias' hand rested on his abdomen, replaying the words over and over in his mind. "You are pregnant." He could sense the anxiety in the room but could not bring himself to focus on the conversation. *Are they worried about my health? Are they scared for our safety? Are they worried about the baby?* He was lost in his own private world, the only thought being that a part of Jonah still lived in him, and he was solely responsible for protecting it.

Just today, he remembered, *my instincts told me to get up off the table and run. Instead of trusting my own judgment to protect the life inside me, I put my faith in my sister who, without fault, could have ended it all. No matter what,* he swore to himself, *I will never give anyone a chance to harm you.*

As he looked around the parlor, where just a few months ago he had stood with Jonah to pledge his love and devotion, Lias could clearly recall each detail of that day. Tears escaped the corners of his eyes as he remembered the transformation that the room had undergone.

He was brought back to the present as he noticed five faces staring at him expectantly, obviously expecting a response. Clearing his throat, he asked, "I'm sorry, what did you ask?"

"Have you been paying attention to this conversation at all?" Eternity challenged.

"Easy," Matthew's soft but authoritative voice interjected. "This is obviously a shock for everyone, especially for Lias. Give him time to process."

"Yes, thank you," Lias replied, grateful for the excuse to delay having to find the words to say.

Samuel moved across the room and sat next to his son on the couch, wrapping him in an embrace. Even though he had a gift for finding the right words to say in any situation, no words could express what he felt at this moment.

Lias was thankful for the silence. He knew that Dad and Papa had had decades to come to terms with the family secret, and what it could mean for the future. His body tensed up under his father's embrace, and Samuel was quick to notice.

"Everyone out now," he commanded, his work voice unmistakable. "You are stressing him out, and I won't allow it."

It wasn't often that Samuel gave orders, but when he did, the family would listen. The four adults in the room, including Matthew, quietly left, leaving Lias and his father in the parlor.

As the room emptied, Lias felt his shoulders relax. He hadn't realized the amount of tension he was unconsciously holding. He leaned into his father's embrace further, grateful to have a dad who always knew exactly what he needed.

Without the noise in the background, and the security of his father's hug, the numbness began to fade and Lias' brain started to wake up. *People are going to notice I'm gaining weight*, he thought. *You can't hide a baby. People will ask where it came from. What if people see Jonah's eyes in the baby? His nose?*

"Dad," he spoke, his mind full of questions.

"Yes?" Samuel answered, tightening his grip.

"What do I do? How can this possibly work?"

"For right now, at this moment, you do nothing," Samuel answered with certainty. "This is not like picking what you want for breakfast while the waitress is standing there tapping her foot. This is something you need to take time with. Think it through completely, and decide what is right for you, and your family."

The words "and your family" resonated in Lias' soul. Samuel had said the one thing Lias needed to hear at this moment. He was no longer alone, but part of a "we."

* * *

Eternity plopped down into a chair across from her father's desk, which was cluttered with massive, dog-eared books. She fumed, "He's being absolutely ridiculous about this whole thing!"

Matthew attempted a chuckle, "Did you expect less? The world's first-ever pregnant man isn't following the textbook behavior for how pregnant women should behave?"

Eternity scowled at him unimpressed. "It's been days, and he won't even let me run any tests beyond taking his temperature and blood pressure!"

Matthew just stared at her, waiting for her to continue.

"He's unreasonably worried that any little test could harm the baby, which at this point I can't even tell if it has five legs and a unicorn horn!" Eternity huffed.

"Well," Matthew finally interjected, "you can't blame him, can you? The first and only test you ran almost led to the extinction of a child he had no idea he was carrying."

Eternity's expression quickly fell as Matthew's words hit her like a ton of bricks. She was suddenly reminded of how close she had come to ending... something. She lowered her gaze to the floor in shame, wondering if her father knew or suspected something.

Matthew noticed her reaction, then softened his tone. "No one can blame you for what you couldn't possibly have known."

Eternity cleared her throat, not wanting the conversation to go any further down this path. "He forgets that this impacts us all. We have all shared in this secret our entire lives. What happens to us all now because of his choices should include input from us all," she said, raising her eyes to meet her father's.

Matthew smiled. "You are your Papa's daughter. I had the exact same thought the first night as I lay in bed, rambling about how Lias needed to take everything more seriously and calculate how the family secret affects us all."

"But you don't feel the same way now?" Eternity asked, catching the implication in Matthew's voice.

"No," he answered, still smiling proudly. "Your father pointed out something to me that I hadn't considered."

Eternity perked up. "What did he point out?"

Just then, Samuel walked in, carrying a tray of tea and crackers. It was as if he had been summoned to the conversation. "I simply shared the flaw in that logic," he began. "You both view this as a branch of the family secret. Where all you children come from is Papa's secret and something we all share a part in. But that doesn't mean that everything from that point on is a branch of that secret."

Matthew smiled at his daughter, watching her try to comprehend the logic being presented.

"This," Samuel continued, "is an entirely different secret. This secret belongs to Lias, shared between him and Jonah alone. We have all been given parts of it, but that doesn't make it ours. Logically, you both assume that this occurred as an effect of Matthew's secret, but you have no way to prove that. This could very well have been a complete fluke of nature that would have always occurred between Lias and Jonah, regardless of Lias' genetic history."

Matthew smirked watching the argument soak into his daughter's mind.

"Clearly, you are versed in playing the devil's advocate..." Eternity began but was quickly shut down by Samuel.

"Clearly," he echoed, "as an academically trained medical professional, you cannot be so arrogant as to assume without tangible facts that what you believe is true in this scenario. If so, your education has been a waste. And since you have been denied access to the information needed to prove or disprove your beliefs, the only logical course of action is to accept what is before you: Lias is pregnant, by some grace of God."

Samuel's words stung Eternity, as they were intended to.

Matthew laughed. "Annoying, isn't he?"

Eternity nodded in agreement.

"But nonetheless, he is right. This secret belongs to Lias, and all we can do as his family is be supportive and offer the best advice we can. But at the end of the day, we cannot be upset if we don't understand his motives or his thoughts. Your grandmother, as supportive a person as I have ever known, may not have agreed with the choices I made to create this family, had she known them. The choices were mine to make, and mine to live with the repercussions of."

"Secret or not," Eternity countered, "a pregnant person should have tests run to ensure everything is going well for the baby and the mother," air-quoting the word 'mother.'

It was again Lias' lawyer who interjected. "Healthy babies are born every day around the world to mothers who have never seen a physician in their lives. For whatever reason, they didn't seek out medical intervention. In our American society, we tend to think of having a family as an event that requires medical intervention at frequent stages, even though our bodies are designed to know what to do without it." Samuel spoke with confidence.

"His body was not designed to do this," Eternity argued.

"Apparently," Samuel concluded, "it is, or it wouldn't be doing it as we speak."

THIRTY-TWO

A **timid knock** on the front door was all it took to rouse Lias from his zombie-like state up from the couch, where he had been spending most waking—and sleeping—hours for the past few months. By the time Lias managed to roll off the couch and totter to the door, the culprit had disappeared, leaving only a small brown box as evidence of their visit.

Lias steadied himself using the door frame as he crouched down and scooped the box under his arm. When he saw the sender's name, an electric shock ran through his weary body. He glanced over his shoulder quickly to make sure he was still alone before reading it again.

Riel. The youthful captain of the *Driftwood*, the boat that had marked the beginning of the end for his husband. *What could Riel possibly have sent me?* Lias wondered. *Why, after all this time?*

Without delay, Lias settled back onto the couch and tore into the tiny box. Inside was an unfamiliar, leather-bound book. Although unfamiliar to him, he knew exactly what it was the moment he saw it. Jonah had always scribbled in similar books, ever since Lias had known him. This must have been the book Jonah had been writing in on the *Driftwood* that fateful June afternoon.

Lias fumbled to open the would-be manuscript and began reading.

Today is a day of irony, Jonah wrote. *As it marks a momentous new beginning in my life and the end of many chapters as an individual.*

I write now, as I often do, to the familiar sounds of my husband's snoring, with sheep dancing above his head in an endless loop. Unlike any other day, today I scribbled with joy, having finally achieved the most exciting feat of my life.

Vowing to this perfect man for me is a goal I never expected to be able to enjoy the fruits of for many decades. Yet here I lay, elated, with an imaginary checkbox ticked as complete. What could I hope for next to surpass the feeling I experience as I splash this page with ink?

I need not be coy with you. As we are one, we both know exactly what we want next. But we both also understand the boundless enthusiasm Lias has for life, and the hundreds of mountains he must climb, rivers he must conquer, and villains he must vanquish before we can dare to dream for the next stage of this story.

One day, when the final candle is lit at the peak of Mount Kilimanjaro, we will be three. We will expand our family. I never imagined the possibility of having a child of my own and Lias', but when Matthew described how he manipulated fate to make it happen for Samuel, I knew before the conversation ended that I would plead with him to do the same for us.

Lias let the book fall to his stomach as his eyes welled up. He had not known before this moment that Jonah was actually writing a journal. Jonah never shared this with Lias. Lias thought back on the thousands of occasions that Jonah was observed writing wondering how many other passages could have also been secret journal entries, and not the characters Lias assumed him to be writing about.

No wonder Jonah never seemed to be scared of the truth about me; he wanted to be part of it. If only he realized from the start that the cards would fall in his favor, and he would get exactly what he wanted without having to ask anyone for anything. The universe was intent on granting Jonah his every wish.

With tears cascading down his face, and Jonah's words etched onto his baby's face, Lias felt fatigue beginning to take over. His interrupted nap was now calling for its imminent completion.

* * *

The stagnant, salty air filled Lias' nostrils as his eyes opened. To his surprise, he was standing once again on the rocky deck of the *Driftwood*—a place that was quickly becoming haunting.

"Rise and shine!" Jonah laughed boisterously from the bridge.

Lias surveyed the scene around him. It was the same boat he remembered, the same sea that still struck fear in his core, but something was different. Jonah was steering the boat instead of its usual aimless drifting.

"What are you doing?" he asked, noticing that his stomach was once again flat like it had been months ago.

"An odd question," Jonah teased. "I'm steering the boat, of course. It's not going to find its way back to shore by itself."

"When did you learn how to drive a boat?" Lias asked, incredulous.

"I've been steering a boat since I was three," Jonah smiled. "I used to peer through the wooden planks at the jungle gym down the street from my house." He continued. "They had a makeshift boat there with a real wheel, and I'd pretend to be a real sailor. I guess it finally paid off."

"I think it'll take more training than fifteen years of playing around a stationary playground," Lias said.

"You may be right there," Jonah admitted. "But since there's no other captain in sight, and you're carrying precious cargo, I'm now the self-appointed captain of this vessel."

As Jonah spoke, Lias watched his stomach grow in seconds to its current size. He admitted aloud for the first time what had been plaguing him for months— "Jonah, I'm scared. I don't know what I'm doing, what I should be doing. I can't do this alone without you."

"Who are you, and what have you done with my fearless husband?" Jonah teased. "You have no problem punching a shark in the face twice, but you're going to allow a little baby to scare the cowardice into you?"

"Well, to be fair, it's more acceptable to punch a shark than a baby," Lias deadpanned.

"I know that," Jonah said. "There's nothing you can't do. I've watched you for more than a decade do anything you set your mind to. All you have to do now is set your mind to being great at this, and you will be."

Jonah's words were always powerful even now, in this dreamscape, he was telling Lias that he was looking at everything backward.

"You're not alone," Jonah reminded him. "You have a huge family right there with you, and I'm right there with you every second of every day."

"It's not the same," Lias said. "I can't feel you with me."

"You can't?" Jonah asked. "You can't feel my presence even now?"

"No," Lias barely got the word off his lips before something pressed hard against his hand resting on his stomach, waking him up to the empty parlor of his childhood home.

It was the first time he felt the baby kick—the first time he had a physical reminder that Jonah was, in fact, right there with him every second of the day.

THIRTY-THREE

As the early morning light spilled across the mound of worn books on his desk, Matthew wiped away the tears from the corners of his eyes— a reminder of the brief moments of sleep he had managed to snatch during the night. The familiar stomping of his oldest daughter on the stairs told

Matthew that Lias was not cooperating with her demands yet again. In the months since Lias had found out about his pregnancy, he had remained firm in his decision not to have any medical tests conducted.

"I can't take it anymore," Eternity exclaimed breathlessly as she burst into the office.

"I take it that Lias didn't wake up any more cooperative than usual today?" Matthew asked with a hint of teasing in his voice.

"Not in the slightest," Eternity replied. "Luckily, Matswell is a more cooperative backup. I'm hoping I can help us figure out how this happened and gather the information I need to make the necessary preparations for the future."

"I'm assuming you didn't waste any time in getting Matswell from the airport yesterday before you started interrogating him?" Matthew queried.

"There's no time to lose," Eternity replied. "We're already years behind in understanding some of the key biological differences between the boys and everyone else."

Matthew propped his chin up in the palm of his right hand, elbow resting on the desk for support. He was eager to hear what revelations his daughter had unearthed after all these years of research. "And what have you found?" he asked.

"I started with basic tests—reproductive DNA," Eternity began. "I won't even tell you how disturbing it was to look at my own brother's semen under the microscope."

Matthew listened intently, regretting the fact that he had given up on searching for biological differences between his children and their peers when they had hit puberty. He leaned forward, eager to hear what Eternity had discovered.

"I found a few things that were easy to miss if you weren't already aware of the boys' ability to get pregnant," she continued.

"And?" Matthew prompted.

"At first nothing unusual showed up under the microscope. So, I decided to run the specimen through a centrifuge, separating it into its components to see if anything stood out. That's when I found something I never expected to find—hiding in the army of sperm was a single egg." Eternity paused for a moment to allow her father to take in the implications of what she was saying. "We collected a second specimen last night and one this morning, and each time the same thing was present—a single egg."

Matthew's mind raced as he was introduced to this new knowledge. *Had I missed something so obvious? Had it been there all along, hiding? Did it develop later in puberty than I had imagined?* A hurricane of thoughts swirled in his mind as he took on the mental responsibility of his youngest son's new situation.

Eternity pulled out some photographic evidence of her findings and pointed out to her father what she had just shared. Matthew held them for a long time, his eyes intently studying them, as if trying to commit them to memory.

The scientist in him kicked in, and he sorted through the overwhelming number of thoughts in his head. "A single egg among an army of sperm—does this mean he impregnated himself?"

Eternity shook her head, an expression of certainty on her face. "No. That was one of my first questions. From what I can tell, they don't even seem to have any interest in each other—like a biological brother and sister scenario, or like magnets with the same charge."

Matthew nodded. "So, then Jonah is a part of this."

"Well," Eternity replied, "I won't be able to confirm that until after the baby is here and I can run proper paternity tests, but all signs point to that being the case."

Eternity had an almost embarrassed look on her face as she continued. "I never wanted to think about the logistics of how the combination occurred."

"We're adults," Matthew countered. "We know how it occurred—the how is irrelevant at this point."

"Right, so," Eternity continued, "I looked at the logistics of everything."

"But neither boy has ever had a period. That would have been noticed by now," Matthew stated with a hint of questioning in his tone.

"Some women have amenorrhea," Eternity offered. "It is an absence of a period, even though they have been through puberty and are not pregnant."

Matthew nodded in understanding.

"I cannot even begin to guess the number of possible reasons for a lack of a period in these two, one-of-a-kind men. But it obviously doesn't impact their ability, or at least Lias' ability to conceive," Eternity started.

"In trying to begin to understand exactly that an interesting puzzle was the hidden biological differences in the twins' bodies," Eternity went on. "In the same way, the throat serves a double purpose for food travel and oxygen exchange, the lower portion of the twins' digestive tracts appears to do the same." She paused, knowing this would invite questions from her curious father.

"Are you saying their anus doubles as a cervix?" Matthew asked.

"No," Eternity replied quickly. "What looks like the anus on the twins is a cervix. Their anus is actually internal, further up the would-be birth canal."

"What?" Matthew asked, his voice shaken with terror. His eyes twitched as he tried to regain control of his body, and he closed his eyes and focused on his breathing until it steadied. "I really messed up," he muttered.

"That's how evolution progresses," Eternity corrected. "Something changes in the genetic line, and then we change over time. In this case, you just helped the evolution along."

Matthew was not soothed by the words. The guilt he felt for what he was apparently responsible for nagged and tugged at his soul, but he pushed those thoughts aside—he would process them when he was alone. For now, there was more to learn about the situation.

Eternity pulled out another image—one that looked like the letter Y with a sharper extension. She pointed at it as she spoke. "Very similar to how the epiglottis functions, here at the intersection," she pointed to the center of the Y, "is where the twins' actual anus is, allowing excrement to share the intended birth canal," she ran her finger down the base of the Y, "to leave the body."

"In the pictures of their ultrasounds, how could I have missed something so obvious?" Matthew pleaded.

"You didn't," Eternity stumbled to capture her father's thoughts before they went off on a tangent. "It wasn't obvious at all. I missed it too until I decided to use a scope—something I would never have done without the knowledge that this could actually happen."

Pointing to the other branch of the Y shape, Eternity continued. "The tuft of the tract is naturally deflated and flat, tight against the digestive tract. You can only see it so clearly here because when I discovered it with the scope, I then inflated it with a surgical balloon to get a better idea of what I was looking at."

Matthew was amazed at the intricacy of the new human male but terrified of the unknowns that now come along with it. "Where is Matswell now?" he asked, finally shifting his mind to his lab rat son.

"He is resting," Eternity answered. "Last night was not fun for him by any means, but as always, he's doing all he can to help get Lias out of the way of his own stubborn choices."

THIRTY-FOUR

Lias fumbled the vibrating phone in his hand. The irritating thud of it hitting the ground below, out of reach, exasperated him. In his current state, there was no hope of retrieving the phone before it stopped ringing. A new plan crossed his mind. He felt around with his bare foot, hoping his big toe could answer and put the phone on speaker.

Surprisingly, luck was on his side, and he managed to do just that.

"Hello," he muttered, groggily, his face planted against the matted seat cushion. Unable to see the number that was trying to reach him.

"Hello Mr. Greene?" a young voice, edged with worry, asked.

"Yes," he answered, trying to focus his movements so as not to miss a word. "This is he. Who is speaking?"

"Sir, this is Leslie from the Bright Star retirement home. I have the unfortunate news that Mrs. Vivian has gone missing, and we have not been able to find her. As per our protocol, we have notified the police and have taken the necessary steps to secure the premises. As a precaution, we wanted to be sure to inform you of the situation as soon as possible."

Is it your protocol to lose loved ones often?" Lias snapped, his instinct getting the better of him.

"No sir, it's not. We are doing everything we can to find Mrs. Vivian, and we wanted to keep you in the loop. We will contact you as soon as we have any updates," the young voice replied, a hint of trepidation in her tone.

"Keep me posted when you do find her," Lias ordered as he slid his toe against the phone once more.

The guilt was already welling up in his chest. He had not thought of Vivian since the news of the baby arrived. How could he forget to take care of Jonah's mom? He knew her son would be devastated.

Lias pushed himself up and off the couch, giving up on the battle to retrieve his phone. He scooted his feet across the floor until he found his slippers and car keys. Vivian's mind was always drifting in and out, but if it was in even a little bit today, there would only be one place she would go.

* * *

The gravel crunched beneath his tires as Lias skidded to a stop in the scorched cemetery. He leaped from the car, calling out for Vivian, but he could not see her anywhere. He stood in the spot he had expected to find her, his eyes closed, weeping until there were no more tears left to cry.

"I'm sorry," he said, his gaze falling on the headstones of Jonah and his father-in-law. "I didn't mean to make such a mess of things. I'm the worst when it comes to forgetting."

"If you're waiting for a response, you may be here a while," a melodic voice teased.

Lias spun around and there she was, Vivian, looking as beautiful as ever. He stepped towards her, giving her an awkward hug with his large belly in the way.

"Vivian, thank God," he exclaimed.

"I thank God every day, love," she smiled. "What has you so upset, dear?"

Dear, Lias thought. *She doesn't recognize me.* While she often used the word dear, it was usually in combination with his name. He knew that something inside of her had led her to this spot, but it wasn't in full control.

"As we all should," he said, forcing a smile. Lias didn't want to alarm her with his confusion.

"Indeed," Vivian said, her eyes falling on his stomach. "Even in the hardest of places, I think you'll find something to be thankful for."

Instinctively, Lias tried to hide his stomach, though he knew it was pointless. His mother-in-law was too senile to recognize the truth, even if she realized it, who would believe it?

"So, what are you doing here, young lady?" he asked, hoping the complimented question would be enough to redirect her attention.

"To be honest, I don't know," she answered. "I was on my way to visit my grandchildren, and something pulled me in." The look of confusion on her face confirmed Lias' suspicions. She wasn't in control of her faculties today.

"They must be worried about you, out here all alone," he said, continuing her delusion. Just then, a familiar car pulled up and Samuel and Matthew stepped out of the black SUV. Before Lias could even ask what they were doing, Matthew held out his hand, revealing Lias' cell phone.

"When we got home, your phone was ringing on the floor. Vivian's home called to say they still hadn't found her, so I guessed you'd come here first," Matthew spoke softly, not wanting to alarm Vivian.

As expected, Lias thought. He was used to his Papa being so logical, with his Vulcan mind. Samuel was quiet in his approach, and by the time Matthew had given Lias his phone, Samuel had already collected Vivian and was guiding her back to the car.

"He'll make sure she gets back home safely," Matthew assured him.

But Lias couldn't move. He watched as Samuel drove away—taking Vivian with him—and he knew Matthew was there to make sure he got back home safely.

"Promise me something, Papa," Lias said, wiping the snot from his nose.

"What is it?" Matthew asked.

"Do a better job looking after her than I did," Lias said, his voice barely audible.

"With everything that's been going on, Vivian slipped our minds," Matthew answered before falling silent. He had a habit of replaying words after they were spoken, and something Lias said lingered in his brain. "Then I did?" Matthew asked. "Are you planning to go somewhere?"

"I wasn't," Lias admitted. "But I am now."

Matthew nodded, albeit tensely. Lias struggled to form the words, especially since they weren't what his audience wanted to hear.

"I've been living the last few months at home under a delusion," Lias said. "I wanted to believe that this baby could grow up in the same house I grew up in, surrounded by the loving family that raised me. But I can't. It's too dangerous. Vivian took two seconds to realize what was going on. If someone *coherent* did the same, the ramifications are unthinkable."

Matthew wanted to yell, to tell Lias to stay with family, where he would have support. But he couldn't bring himself to do it.

"No one can tell you what the right choice is for you and your child," he said, placing his hand on Lias' back. "Yes, I would love it if you and the baby could stay in our home forever. But I won't try to persuade you to make my desired choice when you're doing the best with the hand I dealt you."

"There's nothing to apologize for, Papa," Lias said, his eyes glowing with sincerity. "Because of what you did, I got to experience something no one else in the world has. It's intimidating and scary, but it's also wonderful and amazing. Jonah wanted this. He wanted to ask you to do the same for us someday."

Matthew stared blankly, unable to process what he was hearing. He had been sulking for weeks, feeling guilty for the way his son's life had been turned upside down because of his meddling. Now he found out that not only did Lias harbor no ill feelings, but that Jonah had wanted it. It was a turn of events Matthew hadn't anticipated.

Lias allowed Matthew to take his hand and help him back towards the car. As they walked, Lias continued.

"I love you all, and I appreciate everything that you have ever done, and will ever do for me," Lias said, his voice shaking with emotion. "For my safety, and for the safety of this baby, once it is born, we will have to leave this amazing home."

THIRTY-FIVE

The laughter in the air around them seemed infinite, with no clear beginning or end in sight. Tavia stepped quickly and purposefully, while Eternity's every move felt forced, as if against her will.

"Why are we here?" Eternity questioned her one-track-minded sister. "And why did I let you drag me all the way to the boardwalk when I have Lias to look after?"

"Last I checked, your patient wouldn't even let you touch him," Tavia teased. "Hurry up before we miss our guy."

"Miss who?" Eternity pushed, but her sister was suddenly struck with selective mutism.

The girls pushed through the throngs of people on the boardwalk, Tavia's heavy boots stomping on the wooden planks as they carelessly made their way forward. The salty, trash-filled air irritated Eternity's hypersensitive nose. She already missed the familiar pollen-filled air of their Georgia home.

The chilly air blowing through the boardwalk swayed the scarf wrapped tightly around Eternity's neck. Looking at the barely dressed patrons around them, Eternity felt extremely overdressed in her button-down blouse. Its long lacy sleeves were a comfort against the chill-filled air, although her attire did seem out of place here.

I can't believe I agreed to this, Eternity thought. But she knew why she had; Tavia had a way of getting what she wanted by finding the most creative way possible to make life difficult if you didn't comply. So, when Tavia showed up at the hospital with an overnight bag, Eternity had already lost the battle.

Tavia slowed her stride as they approached the end of the pier, which she had led them to. There, between a two-wheel hotdog vendor and a man offering free hugs, was a man in dark attire, completely out of place among the colorful surroundings. He wore a solid black hat and large dark, tent-like glasses that covered most of his face.

Eternity thought, *This isn't suspicious at all. What is Tavia up to? Is she arranging some kind of secret passage for Lias and the baby? Witness protection for us all? What is her game?*

As she walked closer, the mystery man's image became clearer. He was dressed more appropriately for a foggy morning in London in the 1600s than for a bright day on the boardwalk.

Tavia walked past the man, about fifteen feet, and perched herself on the ledge of the pier, with the shadowy figure at her back. She waited for Eternity to join her at her side.

The both of them stared out at the ocean, with Eternity's heart racing with fear. *How can she be so calm? Is this her daily life?* Eternity knew who her sister worked for, but until now, had no idea what exactly it was that her sister did, aside from hijacking helicopters for bachelor parties.

Tavia brushed her fingers through a small mound of sand that had been piled up on the ledge. From the pile, she pulled out two earwig microphones. She placed one in her left ear and handed the other to Eternity.

"I don't know how you found me, or why," the voice rasped in Eternity's ear, speaking slowly and separating each word. With her peripheral vision, Eternity could see Tavia standing still and unbothered, her gaze fixed on the people running up and down the beach. Eternity attempted to imitate her sister's serene poise, although it was a far cry from the uneasiness that coursed through her.

"That's unimportant now," Tavia responded calmly, her voice betraying no hint of the tension that had built between them. "We didn't come here for me to figure out your motives."

"No," the voice agreed, a hint of irritation creeping into its tone. "We are here because, apparently, some very powerful people owe you a favor."

"It's nice to be helpful," Tavia replied, her words implying a rebuke of the implied accusation. "Do you have something for me?"

"Patience," the voice snapped, and the sisters stood in silence, watching a family of four running after a German Shepard on the beach in front of them.

Eternity could tell that Tavia was getting impatient, as she took a deep breath—no doubt about to make a comment that would only further antagonize the raspy voice in her ear. But before she could, the voice spoke again.

"To your left, use the coin-operated binoculars at 45 degrees north and you will see what you are looking for. There are coins at the base of the lens."

Without a word, Tavia nodded at the binoculars and motioned for Eternity to move five feet toward them. Tavia inserted the coins, and slowly rotated the binoculars back and forth, pausing at intervals.

"Red," the voice hissed, and Tavia found what she had been searching for. She stepped back from the binoculars, careful not to disturb its alignment, and fed more coins into the machine. She motioned for Eternity to look inside.

Eternity stared through the looking glasses, not sure what she was supposed to be seeing. The sun's orange rays were dancing on the sand around them, and Eternity could make out a small boy, no more than three, shoveling sand from a blue bucket into a small tower at his feet. *A sandcastle*, Eternity thought. The boy's mother was watching in amusement, as were several other women.

Eternity felt lost. *Had she accidentally moved the telescope? Had whatever she was supposed to be seeing moved out of focus? How could any of this help them—help Lias?*

The overly excited toddler threw a shovelful of sand into his own face, and his mother knelt to wipe it away with the tail end of her shirt. That's when Eternity saw it—the flowing red hair and young teen's face that were all too familiar to her, having been the source of many of her nightmares. Eternity quickly counted the family around the small boy—nine women in total. She was wrong—this had nothing to do with her family, directly. This had to do with an unsolved mystery of hers, regarding another family.

"Emilia?" Eternity yelled, turning to where the raspy-voiced man had been on the bench.

But when she looked around, the bench was empty, except for an old black overcoat, a large sun hat, and a pair of sunglasses. Eternity searched the crowd for a suspicious-looking figure, but everyone seemed to be enjoying the company of their friends and families. The man with the answers was gone.

"Is that Emilia?" Eternity asked, turning to her sister.

"Yes," Tavia confirmed. "After seeing how shaken you were about the whole situation, I decided to look into the matter myself and see if I could find out what happened to her. I'm not sure why you didn't ask for my help in the first place."

"And how many broken bones did it take for you to find that out, exactly?" Eternity asked jokingly, although she was not completely ruling out the possibility that her sister had resorted to violence.

"The devil is in the details," Tavia smiled smugly. "But the most important part is that she is safe, the baby is safe, and her family is safe."

"What happened to them?" Eternity's voice was filled with questions, her eyes pleading for answers that could put her nightmares to rest.

"Well, as you know, there was potential for civil unrest regarding a modern-day pregnant virgin," Tavia began. "The government obviously couldn't just allow that to get out to the public. Can you imagine how easily the fabric of this country would be torn apart if that got out?"

"So, the government relocated them here?" Eternity asked.

"No," Tavia answered sharply. "Before the government was able to get a plan mobilized and in place, another more organized group swooped in, collected the family, and erased their former existence."

"Who?" Eternity's shaky voice begged for the answers she had been seeking.

"They call themselves the Cleansers," Tavia paused, glancing towards the family that could no longer be seen without the binoculars. "They are made up of liberal-minded military personnel, doctors, lawyers, academics, and even some trustworthy politicians. They're a group who embrace the mysteries of life without the need to solve them all; they just let the secrets be secret. When any natural anomaly occurs, they are the ones who work to protect and hide it from those who would extinguish it—secrets like little Montgomery down there."

"Are you a part of this group?" Eternity asked.

"No," Tavia snapped, "and for the same reason you should never be. When you have secrets to hide, the last people you should spend too much time with are people who make a living from secrets."

The two stood in silence, watching the tide roll in and the sun disappear completely. Eternity's mind was racing with questions, trying to make sense of everything she now knew.

"What's wrong?" Tavia asked, noticing her sister's pain. "I thought it would make life easier for you to know what happened to them. I thought you wanted to know."

"I do want to know," Eternity echoed, distantly. "But I would have liked to know even more before I almost tore an innocent life from Lias' stomach..."

"Well, you didn't," Tavia reassured her. "You took all the information you had available to you and were trying to make the best choice possible, given the circumstances. There was a time when mothers prayed nightly, worrying about their children sailing off the edge of the flat Earth."

"So I'm just as naive?" Eternity sniffled.

"No," Tavia countered. "It makes you a worried mother who was doing everything in her power to save her family. Just as those past mothers worried because they didn't know everything at the time, the same scenario lives today in every choice we make. There is no choice to be made that, if tomorrow's knowledge was available today, would not be changed to some degree."

THIRTY-SIX

A melodic cascade of musical strings being plucked stirred Lias' attention on the oversized couch in the family parlor. He recognized the tune immediately; it was coming from outside the house. A windchime Samuel had constructed when Eternity was very young, from a harpsichord she used to play. Samuel loved the sounds of the harpsichord, but it drove Matthew crazy. When it was no longer playable Samuel had pieces of it made into a wind chime that continued to irritate Matthew.

The windchime's tune changed depending on the direction and force of the wind. On light summer nights, it was a school-kid's whistle as he chased fireflies in the night sky. On days when the wind was strong, the bow of the harpist would slide across the strings in an out-of-breath, high-pitched sound, like a child running away from an older sibling.

But on the rare days when the wind blew in from the east, the tune was captivating, as if a tiny fairy were luring you to a life of play and junk food-filled nights with your best friend.

Tonight's melody was peaceful. The light pricks of the strings tucked into the wooden chimes put a childlike smile on Lias' face and he sat up on the couch, then stood.

Lias sighed as his stomach grumbled loudly like a protective guard dog pacing up and down his fenced-in yard. *It's two in the morning again*, he thought to himself, as he carefully stepped into the kitchen to avoid waking his sleeping parents.

"I really don't get you, my actor," he mused aloud. "During the day, all you want is healthy food—fruits, vegetables, nothing processed or canned. But at night, when no one's watching, you want the worst food imaginable. Are you already performing for an invisible audience? Have you already figured out that the world is a place where you should hide your secrets from public scrutiny?"

He retrieved from the cupboard the ingredients for the baby's go-to midnight snack: two slices of bread buttered on both sides, slathered with crunchy peanut butter, a layer of dill pickles, and a thick slice of raw white onion. "I can barely stomach this for you," he muttered as he put the sandwich together. "But I suppose if this is the worst thing you do to me, I should count my blessings."

Lias took the sandwich outside to the front porch, letting the wind chime serenade him as he hid the awful snack from the sleeping world. As he always did, Lias had to close his eyes and not think about what he was eating in order to get it down. From the past month, he had come to understand that if he didn't give in to the baby's snacking demands every night, he would struggle to feel full all day long, no matter what he ate.

As he closed his eyes, he continued his internal dialogue with the baby. "I don't know about you, but I'm exhausted from all the 'help' everyone is giving us," he thought. "I was under the wrong impression that when someone helps you, it would make things easier. But not in this family. In this family, help comes in the form of pushing you to do stuff you would never make yourself do alone."

Lias faced out into the yard, letting the breeze waft across his soft skin. In just a few hours, Tavia will be over here demanding that we meditate together, do some upper body Tai Chi, and lap the yard. "I love your crazy aunt," he sighed, "but she seems to think that all we need to get through this and make us both healthy are happy thoughts and an exhausted body. Some days I want to tell her to take a hike and get some sleep!"

Lias chuckled under his breath at the thought of his military-trained sister catching wind of him wanting to quit her platoon. "She'd make me do push-ups and then court-martial me," he mused.

"Your grandpa Sam gets my frustration," he continued his internal monologue. "After Tavia's hour of power, he always has a full spread of food waiting on us. I guess he believes that if we're well-fed with four-course meals three times a day, we'll be just fine."

Lias had not yet settled on what to have the baby call his dad Samuel. For his Papa, it was easy; the first night he talked to the baby about its 'Pawpaw,' the name fit Matthew perfectly. But for Samuel, it was not so simple. Every day, he thought of something different, trying to find what felt right. The task seemed daunting, as his list of options was running out. So far, Lias had tested out versions of Grand, Gramps, Pas, Pappy, Pops, Pop Pop, Abuelo, Lolo, Nonno, Babu, and now back to basic Grandpa. Samuel was basic, but unique. Lias wanted to honor that by making sure what his generational name becomes was absolutely perfect. As the first of the kids to have children, whatever he decides would impact all the future grandchildren.

"We barely get to enjoy the great food Grandpa Sam makes before your Aunt Eternity arrives every morning with a barrage of questions about how I slept and my bowel movements, and makes me stand on a scale," he complained. "Every day, she seems to get more and more frustrated that I won't let her do more, and I won't take her vitamins. But after almost losing you before I even knew you existed, I can't take any chances with you. You are one of a kind, and you can't be replaced if I make the wrong choice for you. That's why I let you have whatever food you ask for. I figure no one knows better than you what you need to feel happy and healthy. I suppose she means well, but she's under the delusion that the only thing we need is for me to look good on her charts and for all my body measurements to fit within the lines of normal on her paperwork. But we're far from normal—I can tell you that."

With that thought, Lias finished the last bites of his awful sandwich and opened his eyes. "Your Pawpaw tries to be less intrusive," he thought. "He checks on how I feel throughout the day. Not in a medical way like your aunt, but more like a meticulous scientist documenting everything possible. I think he needs to know for the future. I believe that, for your uncle's sake as well as your own, Pawpaw needs to figure out all the unknown sciences that impact us differently than the rest of the world. Protecting us from science is the most important consideration for Pawpaw in our future."

"Uncle Matswell," Lias continued, "is going to be your favorite—I just know it. Don't go telling your aunts, but he gets me, he gets this, and as soon as he gets the opportunity, he'll get you, too. No ill feelings towards the rest of the family, but he is the one who absolutely understands what you need right now. After everyone leaves for their day and he's had a chance to recover from the battery of tests that Eternity unleashed on him the night before, he comes over and enjoys our company. He makes me get dressed up even though I have nowhere to go and takes pictures of us every day. Not in a study-us way, but in a this is an experience to always look back on way. He reads to you, he sings to you in that awful, off-key, low country voice of his. He tells you stories about your dad, stories that help me remember just as much as they help you to learn about him for the first time. Uncle Matswell knows it's important for you to know the man who would have loved you more than anyone else in the world ever will. Matswell touches you, he feels your kicks, and comments about what he thinks is making you move. While everyone else obviously loves you and wants you to be healthy, there is some obvious fear there. Uncle Matswell treats you like any other baby in the world, not like some rare event. He's already spoiling you. That's how I know he'll be your favorite, and I wouldn't want it any other way. He doesn't know this yet, and neither do you, but if anything ever happens to me, Uncle Matswell will be the one who raises you."

THIRTY-SEVEN

L**ias stared** as his father, Samuel, worked his way around the kitchen, tidying up the holiday-sized meal they had just finished. It felt like Thanksgiving in October, though most of their meals for the past month had been the same.

No matter how hard he tried, tears started rolling down his cheeks as he watched his father work. When Samuel turned to grab the dishes in front of

Lias, he noticed his son's emotion-filled face, holding back the Nile.

"What's wrong, baby?" Samuel asked, pulling up a chair next to Lias.

"How do you do that?" Lias asked, wiping the corners of his eyes with the sleeve of his shirt.

Samuel looked around the room, trying to guess the source of Lias' question. "How do I wash the dishes?" he chuckled. "I taught you how to wash the dishes when you were a little boy."

"But how do you wash them with love?" Lias corrected. "Watching you, it doesn't look like the chore it is when I have to do it."

Samuel didn't answer immediately. Instead, he looked at his teary-eyed son for a moment. "I am so sorry, baby," Samuel said, concern in his voice. "We're all so used to you being so strong and self-sufficient, I forgot that there are things in life you haven't been prepared for. Like how to wash the dishes as a father."

Lias nodded as Samuel hit the nail on the head of what he was feeling. Being emotional over something as trivial as washing the dishes with love was tearing him apart. He didn't want to be that kind of person.

"Well, it's not something I learned in a day," Samuel began, "but I can teach you in a few sentences. It's something I came across by accident, reading some literature in the lobby of the CDC here in Atlanta when your father was applying for his old job. At the time the words didn't mean anything to me, but the day we brought Eternity home from the hospital they dragged themselves up from my subconscious, and I've been changed ever since."

"What was it?" Lias asked, clearing his throat and letting himself be engulfed in his father's memory.

"It was a few statistics; I can't remember the exact numbers, but it was something like 50 million people per year getting sick from foodborne illnesses. Of that, some 200 thousand of them require hospitalization, and several thousand of those die." Samuel said.

Lias raised an eyebrow, trying to make the leap of his father's story. He stayed silent as his father's voice quieted.

"It honestly scared the hell out of me to know that something small, like an unclean kitchen or incorrectly prepared food, had the chance to make the tiny girl in my arms sick or worse. With a secret like this family holds, I knew I had to do everything in my power to make sure it never got to that point.

That night, once I had put her to sleep, I started cleaning this very kitchen, scrubbing everything from ceiling to floor, then again. As you described, I clean with love because love is why I clean. The moment you hold that baby for the first time, so many things are going to change in your life in an instant. A switch is going to click that you had no idea lived within you." Samuel paused to let his words sink in for his overwhelmed son.

"When does the fear of doing something wrong as a parent stop?" Lias asked, his eyes wide and sincere.

"I'll let you know when it does," Samuel smiled, getting back to his feet to finish the task at hand. "There will always be something to be afraid of, something to wish you could protect your child from. As I look at you every day now, I am terrified. But a life with nothing to be afraid of losing is not a life worth having. You will just learn what things you can impact that are the most important and focus your efforts on them. Everything else you have to put faith in the universe to bring you the help you need."

The aromas of sage and baked apples lingered in the air as Lias watched his father clean the rest of the kitchen in silence. Neither minded the quiet. With every dish scrubbed, and every surface wiped and swept, Lias felt a stronger bond with his often-silent father than he ever had before. A layer of protection he never realized was there before this night. *I hope I can be this strong when I have to be.*

The thought reminded him of something he wanted to share with his father at that moment. "I found a few places today to look at buying that will be completely covered by survivor benefits, with enough remaining for us to live on for a long while."

Samuel made his way back across the kitchen with a slice of pie and a tall glass of milk, neither of which Lias asked for. He set them down in front of his son and grabbed a slice for himself.

"Where are you looking?" Samuel asked, sitting down across the table from Lias. This was not a subject Samuel was thrilled to discuss. He wanted nothing more than for Lias to stay here with the baby forever.

"All three very remote towns in the middle of nowhere," Lias said. "It should be easy to go unnoticed there."

"If I may," Samuel asked, and Lias nodded in approval. "Growing up in a small, middle-of-nowhere town, I can tell you that there is no better place to be discovered than a small one. People's lives are so uneventful that they often find entertainment in gossiping about their neighbors, whom they barely know. In a city, you can easily blend in and go unnoticed. People have too much on their minds to worry about the day-to-day lives of strangers. But in the country, it's their mission to know as much as they can about everyone and their pasts."

Lias gazed into his father's eyes, trying to make sense of the words he was hearing. Though they had lived in Atlanta for most of his life, aside from a few months when he was five, Lias had never experienced living in a small town before.

"People notice things and dwell on them," Samuel said, his voice full of concern. "Everyone thought I was gay before I even knew what that meant. The moment I spoke a few words to an unknown gay former student who was sitting next to me at a football game, the gossip mill started. Wherever my family went, people would whisper as we passed by."

"Was there no place safe for you?" Lias asked, "Surely at the school, where people are supposed to be more educated?"

"You'd think so, wouldn't you?" Samuel said with a hint of sarcasm. "But in small-town America, the schoolhouse is the epicenter of gossip and hate. It's often where these things originate and grow."

Lias listened to his father's disdain as he recalled what must have been a very difficult past. At that moment, Lias realized how little he knew about his father's childhood. As he was considering moving his future family to a small town, the first-hand accounts of someone he knew and trusted were invaluable.

"I remember the day vividly," Samuel said, his eyes welling up with emotion. "I was in history class when the elementary school principal—a close friend of my family—peeked her wicked head in the classroom door and asked to see me for a moment. In a real school, this would have been out of the ordinary, but in our small Nebraska town, the principal from across the parking lot had free reign of the grounds."

"What did she want?" Lias asked, his nerves on edge as he waited for the answer.

"She pulled me into the center of the hallway," Samuel said, wiping away a tear. "Within earshot of at least five classrooms, all of which had their doors open that day to let in a breeze. She held me with one hand on each shoulder, gripping me tightly so that she was face to face with me, and I was forced to hear the words she was about to say to me."

Lias, not knowing what those words were, was already crying too, his tears dripping onto the half-eaten pie below him.

"In the middle of the hallway of the small-town schoolhouse," Samuel reiterated, "the elementary school principal held me steady and started to preach to me about how God did not approve of my lifestyle. Before I could even respond to her disapproving words, she began to quote scripture after scripture about how God condemned homosexuality. Her voice carried down the hallway and I started to see heads of teachers and other students peeking out of their classrooms to see who the conversation was directed at. Doors closed and blinds were pulled shut by every classroom. I begged her to believe me that I was a virgin and hadn't had sex with anyone, let alone another boy. It didn't matter—for what seemed like forever she shook my body and condemned me to hell for having a single conversation with the stranger from the football game."

Lias' body shook with anger and sadness as he relived his father's pain. "Why did she not do it in a private classroom? Not that she had any right to have that conversation anywhere with you," Lias asked, his voice trembling.

"She was pompous and, as a family friend, felt it was her responsibility to 'educate' me," Samuel said, air quoting the word. "She also knew there was no way I was going to go home and tell my parents what happened to me that day. As for why she did it in such a public place, I assume it had two reasons. One, to make sure all my peers saw and heard. Small towns love to use peer pressure as a method to make you do or not do something they feel strongly about socially." He paused.

"And number two?" Lias prompted.

"And number two, likely the more important of the reasons, was to allow any other student who may feel different to see exactly what type of ridicule would be bestowed upon them if they decided to act on any non-Christian impure feelings. It's ironic, really, because in the very classroom I was pulled out of, sat the pregnant daughter of the very principal who was lecturing me, ready to give birth to her second child from her third pregnancy."

"How did you move past that?" Lias begged to know.

"Damaged," Samuel replied. "After living through that scene and no teacher or student coming to my aid, I isolated myself. I had no trust in any of the people I passed in the hallway. No peer, and certainly no adult was in that establishment for the purpose of looking after me. Friends no longer sat with me at lunch. Boys would run out of the bathroom if I walked into it. It was a horrible chapter of my life."

Lias stared, tears still streaming down his face, as he empathized with his young father. His wide eyes asked, pleaded, to know what happened next.

"Two days later, I accidentally locked my keys in my car. While I was waiting for a ride home, your father appeared out of nowhere, his first day transferring to the school. We quickly became friends, and then more. It's ironic, really—the whole purpose of that talk was to keep me from being gay, and yet it was the one thing that ended up pushing me into the arms of another man." Samuel attempted to fake a smile.

Lias sat mortified, imagining his son—the spitting image of Jonah—being singled out at a school that way, being subjected to mental torture by an adult in charge of a place where he should be safe from that type of abuse. The image made him instinctively clench his fist and prepare to attack the imaginary principal whom he never met.

Once his emotions had calmed, Lias was able to get back to the topic at hand. "What do I do about moving then?" he asked.

"As much as it pains me to agree with you," Samuel admitted, "you are right—you cannot stay here after the baby comes. At least not for a while. You and Jonah have too many close friends who will have questions you don't have answers to. I think you should find a decent-sized town where you can disappear in plain sight. Ideally somewhere too annoying for close friends to want to see you, but not too far away so that we can still be a part of the baby's life. Then, after a few years, when memories are no longer fresh, you can decide if it is right to stay away or if you feel safe coming back to Atlanta."

Lias nodded in agreement. "Will you help me find such a place?" he asked. "I'm obviously missing the full picture perspective, and this is not a choice I can make lightly."

A loving smile tugged at Samuel's lips. "If I can wash dishes full of love, I can certainly pick a place to live that will be right for you and that baby."

THIRTY-EIGHT

Lias fumbled dropping Jonah's journal he was reading for the hundredth time in the near pitch-dark room as the toll of the grandfather clock began to strike the hour. His stomach quiet, he assumed the baby was still asleep, so he figured he should get up and make the necessary sandwich for it.

Lias reminded himself that it wasn't too many more days until the scheduled C-section. Although he feared the idea of going through another medical procedure, he feared, even more, the unknown of what his body would be able to do naturally, unassisted. He couldn't take that risk, even if it meant his own life. The baby had a better chance of surviving this way.

As he passed the noisy clock that had woken him, something in the darkness on the wall next to the clock called to him. An energy pulled him, as if to say, *Look at me*. Lias fumbled around for the light switch in the hall and was reminded of what hung on the wall next to the mighty timekeeper.

The photo was only a few years old. Lias could feel the excitement as if it were yesterday. This picture was a reminder of freedom, the end of required education. As he scanned the faces of the boys and girls proudly displaying their caps and gowns, he easily found the huge grins of his brother Matswell and, of course, Jonah.

But that wasn't what he was looking for now. Those weren't the faces that beckoned him at this late hour. A second pass through the cluster of bodies and his eyes landed on the only face in the picture that was not smiling, the only person in the class not thrilled to be moving on.

Bobby Brown stood in isolation, not a single part of his robe touched the two unlucky students who stood next to him. His long, dirty curls pushed out from under the cap that was two sizes too small. The clearly pre-worn cap and gown had likely been a hand-me-down from one of his many older siblings. The Brown family kept to themselves, rarely talking to anyone outside their own kin.

Lias had known the boy since kindergarten, but he knew nothing about him. While he could recall some bit of knowledge about almost every single person in the photo, he knew absolutely nothing about Bobby. *How is that possible*, Lias wondered.

It occurred to him that every other student in the photo would have the same trouble recalling anything of significance about Bobby. He now understood exactly what his father had discussed earlier; Bobby was hiding in plain sight.

Whatever secrets this young man had, he had managed to make it through thirteen years next to all these individuals without anyone caring about his life outside of school. The picture started to blur, and a new image entered his mind. He imagined the quiet boy being pulled from his classroom and into the hall to be scolded by the monstrous principal for being different.

Unlike the story his father told over dinner, in this version, as soon as the wicked witch started to scold Bobby for being different, students from the photo, one after the other, filed out into the hallway to stand between her and the outcast.

Lias knew that at least some of the people in the photo would have come to the aid of their classmate, even if they didn't know him. Someone would have stepped in. Lias knew exactly who would be the first to take a stand for the strange boy. The imagined scene disappeared as Lias stared at Jonah's face. His hero.

* * *

Matswell closed the book he was reading to the baby, and their daily routine was complete as he placed a hand on Lias' stomach and received the expected high-five from his favorite person in the world. A wide grin spread across Matswell's face.

"I've been meaning to talk to you about something," Lias whispered.

"Is it the baby's name? Are you finally going to tell me?" Matswell asked, beaming with excitement.

"No," Lias answered for the thousandth time. "You'll know when I tell everyone, after the baby is here."

"Well, if it's any more tests you want me to run in your stead, then count me out. Our sister has already given me a thorough check-up without even buying me a drink first," Matswell joked.

"Nothing quite as invasive as what she's done to you. I'm sorry about that, by the way," Lias apologized. "But, yes, this is a test of sorts."

Matswell raised a questioning eyebrow and sat up on the couch, having been crouching in front of his soon-to-be niece or nephew.

"It'll all be over in just a few days," Lias reassured him. "And if anything should happen to me during… I want you to raise the baby in my place. You have the closest bond to him, and if neither of his fathers can be there for him, at least his favorite person in the world can be there for him."

"I'm his favorite person in the world?" Matswell asked, his face lighting up. "How do you even know it's a boy?"

"Just a feeling I get," Lias answered. "No girl would want to eat the things he makes me eat at night when no one's looking." He paused. "So, will you?"

"I'll always be here to look out for him, in whatever capacity necessary. But you have the best surgeon in Atlanta at your disposal. Nothing is going to go wrong," Matswell reminded him. "So, enough of this silly 'what if' talk," Matswell said, a chill running down his spine. "It's a waste of time. Everything is going to be just fine."

Lias stared into Matswell's eyes, into his soul, but did not speak.

"Fine, fine I will," Matswell conceded. "Enough with the Jedi mind tricks already. That should at least give me access to the name before everyone else."

THIRTY-NINE

Lias awoke in the middle of the night, as he was accustomed to. His stomach cramps were much stronger than usual, and he knew the baby must be really hungry. "I hear you, I hear you; I'm going," he muttered, as he reached down to propel himself off the couch.

Suddenly, he felt the damp cushion beneath him and realized his shorts were wet too. *This must be it*, he thought, recognizing the signs of his water breaking. "I guess you have no plans to wait another week, do you?" he asked, wincing at a sharper throbbing in his abdomen.

He felt around in a panic for his phone, only to find it had fallen to the floor again. "Dad, Papa!" he yelled. "I think... I know the baby is ready to go!"

At the sound of his voice, a flurry of activity echoed from the other side of the house. Something crashed to the ground and broke. Then, Matthew burst into the parlor, flipping on the lights. Lias squinted against the sudden glare.

"Are you sure?" Matthew asked.

"Well, my water broke," he teased, trying to make light of the situation. "I think that is a pretty good start. Don't you think?"

But Matthew was staring at the puddle of blood on the floor, the blood-soaked couch, and the red-stained white shirt covering Lias' stomach. "Your water didn't break," he corrected.

Lias looked down to realize that his father was right. The wetness he felt in the dark room was in fact blood, and it was everywhere.

"Tell Eternity it's a 911," Matthew yelled up the stairs to Samuel, who already held his phone to his ear, speaking frantically. "I don't think we can wait for her to get here; I think we need to get you to the hospital now."

"No," Lias growled, wincing as another cramp pulsed through him. He could feel the blood running down his leg like a blood-filled orange being squeezed to the max. "We have a plan in place, we're just going to have to execute it sooner than we planned."

"Lias, you have lost a lot of blood, and you are pale as a ghost," Matthew argued. "This is more important than..."

But Lias cut him off. "No," he insisted. "It's my choice."

Matthew sighed, his eyes narrowing as he looked down at the blood dripping from his son's ankle. "It is," he hissed through clenched teeth, "but you are making the wrong one." He leaned down to help Lias, who was struggling to stand. "Come on," he said softly. "Let's get you to the hospital."

"Enough," Samuel's stern voice boomed. "Get him downstairs. Eternity will be here in fifteen, with Matswell. Tavia is clear across town, but my bet is she makes it before them."

Samuel and Matthew walked on either side of Lias, with his arms draped over them. He could only take a few steps at a time, as his burning muscles threatened to tear him apart from the inside. By the time they got him settled into the home clinic in their basement, the squealing tires in the driveway announced that someone had made it.

Lias was just laying back on the cold aluminum table when Matswell and Eternity ran through the door. Eternity was barking orders around the room, and everyone scattered, but Lias could not make out the words being said. He felt his mind drifting out of consciousness, even though he had not been given anything that should have made him drowsy. *I am dying*, he thought. *This must be what it feels like.*

"Mats, Dad," he called with a voice barely over a whisper.

Samuel, who had sequestered himself into a corner and out of the way, dashed to his son's side.

"Mats," Lias spoke. "Remember, if anything happens to me, I want you to raise the baby. That is my wish, Dad. Please make sure."

Tavia flew across the room, pushing between her dad and Lias. "Tavia," Lias smiled. "Save the baby, not..." Before he could finish the sentence, Lias fell unconscious.

The room was full of frightened faces as everyone overheard the exchange. Not only was Lias certain he was not going to make it, but there was already a backup plan in place to ensure the baby lives and who would care for it. No one in that room would dare cross Tavia. Matswell reached down and held Tavia's hand in solidarity. Even if anyone dared challenge her, with Matswell on her side it would take a small army for anyone to act outside of Lias' orders.

* * *

"There he is," Jonah chuckled. "Good afternoon sailor."

Lias reflexively scanned his surroundings, the rocking of the *Driftwood* making him queasy. "If you don't do something about that rocking, you'll soon have to swab the deck, sir," he said.

"Now is that any way to talk to your captain?" Jonah teased.

"The baby," Lias remembered, instinctively reaching down to feel his now flat, uninhabited stomach. "I must have died. Is this heaven?"

"Is your memory that bad, my love? This is the *Driftwood*. I think heaven would need a much bigger boat and a more experienced captain, perhaps a first mate or two… thousand," Jonah laughed.

"I think I did die. But don't worry, the baby is in more than capable hands," Lias reassured.

"I'm sure that's true," Jonah agreed, "but no hands would be more capable than his fathers."

Jonah returned to his station at the wheel. Lias followed, staring off into the endless sea before them.

"Where are we headed, captain?" Lias asked, wrapping his arms around Jonah as he stood tight behind his husband.

"Well, I'm headed out to explore all that the vast sea has to offer, to experience all the adventures unknown to those who keep their feet firmly on the ground. There are thousands of stories out there just waiting for me to come along and write them," Jonah's face lit up as he talked about all the stories he would soon be writing.

"Sounds great," Lias agreed.

"It will be, my love. Sadly though, you're not invited. We're almost at your stop."

"At my stop? We're in the middle of nowhere," Lias said as the *Driftwood* crashed to a halt. He tried to grab onto Jonah, who no longer stood at the helm of the ship. The great force of the boat hitting land flung Lias backward, head over heels he tumbled over and over again until the space to tumble through the ship ran out and he struck his head on the stern before being tossed out to sea.

FORTY

Lias **awoke** to the sound of shuffling in the room, the light so bright he could not open his eyes fully. His brain felt foggy. *Some type of medication*, he imagined. As he slowly cracked them open, he saw Samuel sitting by his side, gripping his hand. His father's red-rimmed eyes were enough to tell him that tears had been shed.

"He's awake!" Samuel exclaimed, squeezing Lias' hand.

Eternity, who had been at the cabinet moments before, rushed to his side. "How are you feeling?" she asked. "You lost a lot of blood, but I expect you to make a full recovery."

Lias' first thought was of the baby. "Is he okay?" he asked, anxious.

"Yes, he's perfectly fine," Matthew said, entering the room carrying a sleeping infant. He stood on the opposite side of the bed from Samuel and Eternity but didn't offer the baby to Lias.

"And, not that you asked," Matswell's deep voice boomed from the doorway, "she's perfectly fine too."

Matswell held a second baby, the beaming smile of an uncle with full intentions of spoiling the little girl. He stood next to his father and tucked the infant under Lias' left arm. Without a word, Matswell gently retrieved her brother from Matthew's strong grip and tucked him under Lias' right arm.

Twins. Lias thought to himself, suddenly understanding his bipolar food cravings. He was overwhelmed with fear and joy. He had two perfect copies of Jonah's best attributes sleeping in his arms.

"Where is Tavia?" Lias asked.

"She went to the store for smaller diapers," Matswell answered. "The ones we have are way too large for these two."

"Are you sure?" Lias asked, worried. "She's not going to walk through that door with another baby any minute, is she? I don't think I can handle any more."

Matswell laughed. "Rest assured, there are only two. I checked in there myself before Eternity stitched you up to make sure she got them all."

Lias' tear-filled eyes gazed down at the two lives he had created. "So, which one of you is the healthy eater, and who is the junk craver?" he asked them.

"My money is on the girl being the healthy one," Tavia said, entering the room with two large bags. "She already looks ready to kick his little butt."

"No way," Matswell challenged. "She's already a little piggy, look at her!"

"He, she," Matthew replied. "Lias, can you please give us their names already so we can have something besides 'boy' and 'girl' to call them? All I've heard for the last few hours while you rested was 'baby girl' and 'baby boy'. I'm ready to know what to call them."

Even though he held two babies at each of his sides it was now really settling in that there were two of them. Maybe the medicine was quickly fading from his system making him more aware. The idea of twins was never considered even though the possibility was there, him himself being a twin.

A name was already picked out for a boy or a girl, but having one of each was a naming possibility

Lias did not see possible before now presented itself. In addition to revealing the babies' names. It was time for Lias to reveal the grandparents' titles.

Lias motioned for Matswell to pick up the baby boy in his left arm. "Opa Sam," he smiled, knowing at the moment it was the perfect fit for him. "I'd like you and everyone to meet your granddaughter, Jo Saphany Greene."

Samuel reached out to take Jo from Matswell. "It's a pleasure to meet you, young lady," he said proudly.

Matswell walked around the bed again, retrieving his nephew without needing to be prompted. "Pawpaw," Lias said, "I'd like you and everyone to meet Noah Matswell Greene."

* * *

The parlor buzzed with life. The family beamed around the enormous Christmas tree, adorned with pink angels and bow-drawn cupids. Eternity plucked away at the piano, and Tavia sang along. Lias lay upon the familiar couch and watched his two fathers each rocking one of their sleeping grandbabies. Matswell snapped photos of every moment.

Though the song was soft, tears escaped from Lias' eyes. The only thing missing in this perfect moment was Jonah. Lias reached into the crevices of the couch to retrieve the recently delivered journal of Jonah's final thoughts. He held the small book tightly against his chest, thinking: *How will I ever do this without you? How will I ever do this without your help?*

Immediately, guilt stabbed him. The words reverberated in his head like a high-pitched bell echoing off granite mountains. *I did it again. As I sit here feeling sorry for myself, across town Vivian sits in a nursing home, completely alone. That is not what Jonah would have wanted—for her to be all alone on Valentine's Day.*

* * *

Matswell followed Lias' quick pace, pushing the double stroller, as they raced through the desolate halls of Vivian's nursing home. The sparse staff, the dust-coated decorations, and the cobwebs that hung from the ceiling made it seem more like a Halloween scene than a place for healing.

When Lias announced his sudden desire to take the kids to visit Vivian, an unspoken protest arose from the room. Matswell, being the most understanding of them all, immediately offered to accompany Lias and take on the task of carrying the twins. Nobody could argue that tireless Uncle Matswell was not the ideal candidate for such a job.

"Good morning," Lias said, as he entered Vivian's room and hastily thrust a gift box into her hands. "Better late than never." Lias silently thanked his father Samuel for always making sure Vivian had presents, even if they were a bit late.

Confused, the old woman turned from her window-facing chair and accepted the box. She pulled out a vibrant multi-colored wool scarf and matching gloves.

"Well thank you, dear," she said.

Vivian has no idea who I am, Lias thought, *grateful for the day*.

"Well, this is exactly what I needed. It has been getting a bit chilly on my afternoon strolls along the canals. H-how did you know?" Vivian asked, her eyes twinkling with joy.

Canals huh? I guess she's in Italy now. "Well," Lias began. "I know how much you love that fresh pasta, and I knew you wouldn't let a little cold weather stop you from getting what you love."

Vivian's lips curved into a grateful smile, one that showed her appreciation for someone who understood her.

"Prices keep getting higher and higher every time I go to the market. It's going to be too expensive soon," she said.

"We can't have that now, can we?" Lias replied.

Vivian then shifted her focus to the silent children in the stroller, sleeping peacefully. "I've been so worried about them."

Though he was used to her frequently changing stories, Lias was taken aback by this comment. *Oh, right*, he remembered, *their last encounter in the cemetery she had mentioned her grandchildren.*

"These last five weeks have been quite nerve-racking for me, waiting to know they are okay," Vivian murmured, as she gently caressed Noah's cheek. "So, who do we have here?"

"That is Noah," Lias said, radiating with a father's overflowing pride. "The pudgy one behind him is Jo."

"Jo, Noah," Vivian repeated. "Jonah would have loved that. He wanted a family so badly, I thought it would break his bones."

At the mention of Jonah's name, fear and dread raced through Lias' body, electrifying every nerve along the way.

"Why do you say that?" Lias asked, his voice trembling.

Vivian's posture tensed. She was leaning over, running her palm over Jo's head, as Lias asked the anxious question. "The market was out of the shells I liked last time. Do you think you can keep your eye out for some? I love them covered in red gravy."

Lias glanced up to the door, noticing Matswell had stepped in. Something in the conversation must have grabbed his attention. In true twin fashion, and without saying a word, Matswell picked up his phone, and then disappeared down the hallway to find the shells and sauce Vivian longed for.

I guess it was just a coincidental comment in a lucid second. This was not the first time Vivian had made a comment that led to questions that could never be answered. A frustration that used to annoy Jonah to no end. Lias was well-versed in smoothly transitioning the conversation, as Vivian liked to do.

"I'm sure we can locate some pasta for you," Lias assured her. "Somewhere in Italy, there has to be a steady-handed Nona rolling out shells and simmering sauce as we speak. I'll find some for you."

"Thank you, dear," Vivian smiled, straightening up as she tucked the blanket tighter around Jo. "I think I should rest now, Lias," Vivian said softly. "Thank you for coming to see me, and for the beautiful scarf."

"You're welcome, Mama," Lias answered, stepping forward for a long, tear-filled hug.

As they embraced, Matswell silently rolled the stroller out of the room.

"Goodbye," Vivian said, as Lias pulled away, tears still dripping down his cheeks.

"We'll see you soon," Lias replied.

"Goodbye, my dear Lias," Vivian echoed.

FORTY-ONE

Lias lingered at his newly purchased dock, gazing across the rippling water at the majestic snow-capped mountains in the distance. He silently thanked his father for this perfect property, which was the only one he had looked at that was close to natural water. When Samuel pitched the idea to his son, he pointed out that Jonah had loved the water and would have wanted his children to be just as connected to it.

In this solitary moment, Lias was glad he had listened to the sound advice of his thoughtful father. Everything about this secluded property was perfect.

The closest town was large enough for the kids to get lost in the masses when they were old enough to start school. Lias smiled, knowing that in this lake his babies would learn to swim and sail a boat, in the mountains they would learn to hike and be one with nature, and in the woods surrounding the entire property, they would learn to live off the land. Exactly what Jonah would have wanted.

In the wind that blew off the lake, Lias could feel Jonah's comforting embrace, reassuring him that this was exactly where he belonged. This was his home.

Lias started the long walk back to his new house where his family was preparing for the drive back to Atlanta. As the tiny house on the horizon slowly grew larger, a few tears escaped his eyes. He had time to dry them before anyone saw him.

Lias wasn't excited about the idea of being so far away from his family. But he knew this was what his children needed to be safe, and he couldn't expect his family to uproot their lives for him. He was the patriarch now and it was his time to step up and be the rock for a new generation. In the wind, he was reminded that he wasn't alone, Jonah was all around.

"There he is," Tavia exclaimed as Lias reached the front yard where suitcases were being loaded into two of the four parked cars. "I had my bets that you were dumb enough to jump into that lake."

"Not till it's at least a few degrees warmer," Lias joked back. "I'm not a fan of swimming with icebergs."

"Good to know," Matthew chimed in as he climbed down from installing the last of the security cameras. He had spent the last two days filling the property with them. "And just in time too. You know how your sister is about being on schedule and apparently, we're scheduled to depart as soon as she gets back from her errand. She's 15 minutes out."

Matthew returned the ladder and disappeared into the house with his mess.

"I'll be back this weekend," Matswell announced, rolling toward Matthew's SUV with the last of his luggage. "And likely every weekend until forever."

Lias smiled, then hugged his brother firmly, choking back the tightening in his throat.

As Lias released Matswell to stow his bag and climb into the car, the procession began. His father Samuel was next up with a bag in hand.

"We're just a red-eye away, baby. If you need anything, we will be here," Samuel assured him.

Lias' knees shook as the two powerful sentences escaped Samuel's lips, threatening to knock him to the ground. Seeing the eruption that was threatening to occur, Matthew stepped up, pulling Lias and Samuel into a circle hug. "I love you, son," he said, as he towed Samuel and their bounty to the car.

The crunching of gravel and the cloud of dust being kicked up announced Tavia's return. Lias just finished drying away his tears when he realized what his wild card of a sister carried in her arms.

"You really think that with two infants, the one thing I need now is a puppy?" Lias asked.

"He won't be a puppy for long. Out here in the middle of nowhere, you need a good, dependable dog—or two—to help keep an eye on the family."

Lias smiled and hugged his sister, thankful that, as always, she was the least sentimental. All business with her, no emotional breakdown today. The squirming German Shepherd now cradled in his arms helped to lighten the severity of the moment.

As Tavia walked away, Eternity was walking back from her car, towing a bag in the wrong direction.

"Forget to pack something?" Lias asked, as his new companion licked away dried tears from his near-frozen face.

"Not at all," Eternity exclaimed. "Do you expect me to leave my stuff in the car?"

Lias stared at her in confusion, as the statement made no sense to him.

"Do you really think I'm going to let you live off-grid here with my niece and nephew alone?"

Eternity asked. "Where will you find a doctor way out here as familiar with their unique situation as me?"

She's staying, Lias realized, as he heard the tires of two cars grind the gravel as they drove away. *Everyone knew but me.*

"What about your job, your patients?" Lias asked as the dam broke, and the eruption of water flowed past the floodgates of his eyelids down his face.

"We don't live in the stone ages, Lias," Eternity confirmed. "The hospital will find another surgeon, and my general practice will be managed day-to-day by the same staff as they always have. I will consult through telemedicine. For the things that need a physical doctor, I decided to share my practice with a new, up-and-coming physician. She is going to do great things in her career, I believe."

"Why?" Lias asked. "Why give up everything for me? For us?"

"I'm giving up long hours, anxiety, and frozen dinners, I think I'll survive."

Lias allowed himself to fall into his sister's capable arms, with his new puppy between them. The weight of the world lifted off his shoulders in a mere second. His babies would be well cared for by one of the brightest medical minds in the world. *I won't be alone.*

"What will you name it," Eternity asked stepping back to look at the busy puppy in her brother's arms.

Lias held him out, both hands gripping him firmly to take in the puppy from a distance. The tiny young thing with deep bronze pelts and a fluffy black mane brought up a single familiar face. A young man Lias will never be able to forget. *It is only fitting*, Lias thought.

"His name," Lias corrected, "is Riel."

* * *

With the babies sound asleep and Eternity settling in, Lias relaxed in a well-worn wooden rocking chair that had come with the place, in front of the crackling, warm, and peaceful hearth. Lias opened the time-worn final words of Jonah as he peacefully rocked himself and Riel.

Today is full of awe-inspiring brilliance. As familiar harbors fade away and the enormity of the open world engulfs me, I am certain of two things: 1) Today is sure to be a day that will alter the trajectory of my life forever, and 2) I wouldn't have it any other way.

THE END.